Dancing Queen

A Connor Maxwell Mystery

DANCING QUEEN
A CONNOR MAXWELL MYSTERY BOOK 3

TIMOTHY GLASS

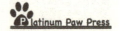

CONTENTS

Other Books by Timothy ix
Acknowledgments xiii
Quote xv

Chapter 1	1
Chapter 2	5
Chapter 3	9
Chapter 4	12
Chapter 5	19
Chapter 6	21
Chapter 7	28
Chapter 8	34
Chapter 9	41
Chapter 10	46
Chapter 11	51
Chapter 12	58
Chapter 13	65
Chapter 14	71
Chapter 15	78
Chapter 16	87
Chapter 17	94
Chapter 18	99
Chapter 19	106
Chapter 20	113
Chapter 21	121
Chapter 22	128
Chapter 23	137
Chapter 24	143
Chapter 25	150
Chapter 26	156

Chapter 27	163
Chapter 28	169
Chapter 29	175
Chapter 30	182
Chapter 31	189
Chapter 32	195
Chapter 33	200
Chapter 34	207
Chapter 35	213
Chapter 36	221
Chapter 37	229
Chapter 38	237
Epilogue	244
A Message from Tim	247
About the Author	249
Visit us on the Web	251

This book is a work of fiction. Any similarity or resemblance to any person, living or deceased, names, places, or incidents is purely coincidental. The work is from the author's imagination. All rights reserved. No part of the book may be reproduced, stored, or transmitted by any means such as electronic, photocopying, recording, or scanning without written permission from the publisher and copyright owner. The distribution of this material, by any means over the Internet or copying of this book without prior written permission from the publisher and the copyright owner, is illegal and punishable by law. Platinum Paw Press appreciates your support and respect of the author's rights.

Dancing Queen

Written by Timothy Glass

Copyright (C) 2020

Cover art by Timothy Glass

Library of Congress Control Number 2020915765

Platinum Paw Press

ISBN 978-1-7331972-2-9

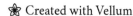 Created with Vellum

OTHER BOOKS BY TIMOTHY

Nonfiction
Just This Side of Heaven
Fiction
Deception, A Connor Maxwell Mystery Book 2
In a Split Second, A Connor Maxwell Mystery Book 1
Dog Knows Best
Postcards
Sleepytown Beagles, Doggone It
Sleepytown Beagles, In The Doghouse
Children's Fiction
Sleepytown Beagles, Panda Meets Ms. Daisy Bloom
Sleepytown Beagles, Penny's 4th of July
Sleepytown Beagles, Oh Brother
Sleepytown Beagles, Differences
Sleepytown Beagles, The Lemonade Stand
Sleepytown Beagles, Jingle Beagles
Sleepytown Beagles, Up, Up and Away

DEDICATION

To all the search and rescue workers around the world who work countless hours and donate their skills and time to help find and bring home the missing and lost. For those who help behind the scenes by setting up camps, coordinating maps, and having hot coffee and cold drinks for the rescue workers, thank you.

ACKNOWLEDGMENTS

Thank you to everyone who helped bring this book from page one to the finish.

QUOTE

I became insane, with long intervals of horrible sanity.
Edgar Allan Poe

Sundae

CHAPTER 1

He stood in the post office lobby after hours, looking through the large plate glass window of the old yellow brick building. He had just spent the better part of the evening and the early morning drinking beer and watching TV in the smoke-filled dive next to the post office. From his vantage point, and fueled by a belly full of liquor, he found that the little reddish-blonde-haired girl across the street was looking better by the minute. She was dusting the shelves and restocking products. Bending down and then straightening up. She wore tight-fitting faded jeans, white blouse, and Western boots. Whatever she was doing now, she was no longer behind the counter.

He had been watching her for the last thirty minutes. Her rhythmic movements almost mesmerized him. She bent over, took something from the box at her feet, straightened up, and then placed the product carefully on the shelf before repeating the process. He cleared his throat several times, a nervous habit he'd had since high school, when he'd been a gawky, pimply-faced teenager. At age sixteen, he'd watched the girls walk by him in the hallways but he was too shy to talk to them. If a girl had seen him looking at her and stopped, he'd just clear his throat, unable to say anything. Inevitably, the girl would giggle and burst into laughter, leaving him standing with his mouth agape. He shook his head as if to erase the memories of those girls and their laughter.

"She's different," he said under his breath as he pushed open the lobby door and walked across Main Street to get a loaf of bread. He needed bread, didn't he? If not bread, he could get a cup of coffee before the walk home. At the edge of the asphalt, he thought again, second-guessing himself. Go home? Or go into the store? Looking both ways, he crossed the street, as if his own legs had made the decision for him.

At this hour of the morning, Main Street in Lakewood looked like a ghost town. In fact, the parking lot of the twenty-four/seven convenience store, called Joe's by the locals, was devoid of any cars except a run-down, blue four-door Chevy. He figured it belonged to the pretty reddish-blonde girl who worked there.

A door chime announced his entrance. Lacey looked up and greeted him with a warm smile. "Hello. Welcome to Joe's," she said in a sweet, soft voice as the lone man walked into the store. Out of habit, she glanced at the pumps. No car was there. Only her old Chevy, sitting at the curb. *He must be on foot. Odd for this hour*, she thought.

The man smiled back at her with a toothless grin and cleared his throat. He tried to say something but the words wouldn't exit his mouth. Lacey turned her attention back to the shelf. She leaned over and picked up an empty cardboard box, then discarded it in the back room. Seconds later, she returned.

"Is there something I can help you find?" Lacey asked as she worked her way back toward the cash register. *At least there I have a panic button if I need one*, she thought. The store had no cameras, despite the fact that, for months, employees had been asking management to install them for their safety and protection.

She watched the man walk down the aisles. He stopped and looked at several things, then walked back toward her before heading to the coffee bar at the back of the store. There, he stood and continued to look at her. His gaze made her uncomfortable and the hair on the back of her neck stood on end. *Is it the hour or just the man himself?* she thought.

Lacey heard him fill a cup of coffee, which he

brought to the cash register. "Will that be all for you?" she asked.

"Yes," he managed to say. He cleared his throat several times and nodded nervously, without a smile.

Lacey smiled and rang up the purchase. The man paid and quickly left. Lacey watched him walk through the front door and head north on Main Street until he was out of sight. She breathed a sigh of relief. The odor of sweat and liquor lingered long after he had left the store. Lacey grabbed a can of room freshener, hoping to rid the store of the smell.

CHAPTER 2

Lacey Warner had been married, had three children, gotten divorced, and become a single parent before her twenty-first birthday. She was a hard worker. She had no choice, as it was the only way to put food on the table for her children and pay the rest of her bills. Lacey lived in a modest, single-wide trailer house that had seen better days.

Her ex-husband, Kyle Warner, suffered from a condition that Lacey liked to call "deadbeat dad memory syndrome." He forgot the first of each month, when the time came to make his child support payments. The fact was, he had pretty much forgotten his three children altogether. Lacey could count on one hand the number of times when, after their divorce, the children had seen their father. Kyle was too busy partying with his girlfriends and shooting pool with his buddies.

When they were married, Kyle and Lacey had gone to country-western dances and partied with their friends. Lacey could line dance with the best of them. One night, Kyle had said she was a regular dancing queen. However, the partying had stopped after their first child was born. Lacey left those dancing days behind. After she became a parent, the only dancing Lacey did was across their tiny living room, trying to quiet one of the kids. Kyle seemed stuck in his teenage years, unable to let go of the carefree life of a single man. He found any excuse to get out of the house. To Kyle, the kids were like a heavy anchor around his neck, holding him back and dragging him down. Having fathered the children was one thing. Being a real dad was another. It simply wasn't in his DNA. He had more important things on which to spend his money and time.

After the third child was born, Kyle was gone. Lacey's best friend from high school, Sofie Lynch, told her that Kyle was living with a girlfriend he'd been seeing at the dances. When he didn't come home and Lacey hadn't heard from him in six months, she scraped together all the money she could and filed for divorce. Her attorney had to send the papers to Kyle's mom's house, as no one knew where the girlfriend lived, or even if he was still dating her.

Lacey had time only for work and taking care of the kids. A friend helped out with babysitting, which allowed Lacey to work the graveyard shift at Joe's Family Convenience Store. It took a while for her to adjust to the hours, but after a month or so, she was getting used to the after-hours clientele. In fact, she looked forward to most of them coming in and chatting with her. Joe's served hot coffee for the late owls, while other people stopped in for gasoline. Plus, they always had snacks for the late-night munchies people seemed to get.

The worst part of the job was when the night gave way to the early hours of the morning and Lacey was the only one in the store for hours. She busied herself dusting and stocking shelves until the early crowd came in before work, filling up with gas, coffee, and pastries for their morning commute. The early crowd wasn't as chatty. Lacey assumed that half of them were simply going through the motions until their coffee kicked in.

Several nights passed before he wandered into the old dive again. He took a seat at the bar and ordered a beer, then watched the old TV that hung from the wall. A woman sat beside him and ordered a beer. He tried to get up the nerve to make conversation and cleared his throat several times until she glanced over at him. The woman refused to engage in any dialog with him. Instead, she moved to the far end of the bar.

Anger and rage rose up in him and he could hear the long-ago laughter of those teenage girls. He looked at the old wooden clock on the wall. The bar would be closing at two o'clock, in an hour, so he slid the empty glass to the edge of the bar, where it joined the other three he had polished off earlier. He belched loudly and smiled at the woman, who rolled her eyes in disgust.

CHAPTER 3

The morning air was brisk – not as cold as it had been when he'd lived in Massachusetts, where he'd done stints in two mental hospitals. Thanks to his father and his money, his attorney had made sure he wouldn't serve any time for either of the cases on which he'd represented him. Once in the mental hospital, all he'd had to do was tell that stupid head doctor what she wanted to hear. He had her eating out of his hands. After his release, he hopped on a bus and headed out west. Maybe a change of location would be good, his father told him, a place where his past wouldn't dictate his future.

"Clean yourself up, Colin. I bought you new clothes." His father motioned to the large duffle bag at his feet. "Find a dentist out west and I'll pay for the dental work. I put a new toothbrush, shaving things, and deodorant in the bag. But you have to use them or they'll do no good. You understand?"

His father had then bought him a one-way ticket to Lakewood. Once there, he'd called his father and asked him to wire the landlord five hundred dollars a month for an old one-bedroom, one-bath mobile home. The landlord hadn't done a background check when his dad had wired a year's advance payment for the home.

He ambled over to the post office lobby. In the dim light, he watched the young reddish-blonde girl, whose back was to him as she put canned goods on the shelf. Each time the young woman bent over and reached into the box on the floor, he leaned closer to the window to get a better look. He smiled, almost hypnotized by the sight. Then he walked outside. He quickly crossed Main Street and burst through the front door of the store.

He ran toward Lacey. Before she had a chance to look up and turn around, the man had grabbed her around the neck from behind. She fought as hard as she could to break free, but it was no use. The man was too strong.

"You can have the money!" Lacey said, barely able to speak due to his tight grasp around her throat. She twisted and turned in an attempt to break free.

She stomped down as hard as she could on the arch of his foot.

"You bitch!" he yelled at Lacey, never letting go of her.

His smell was so overpowering and nauseating that she thought she would vomit. She wasn't sure if it was his smell, her panic, or both. He pulled her across the store to the cash register.

"Open it!" he demanded.

Lacey opened the register. With his free hand, he pulled out all the bills and stuffed them into his pocket.

"That your car out there?" He pointed to her old car in the driveway, almost lifting her off her feet.

"Yes, just take it, please! I have three children at home. Please!" Tears filled her eyes and spilled down her cheeks.

He pulled her away from the register and to the home goods section. There, he grabbed duct tape and pushed her onto the floor. He straddled her and his weight on her petite frame was almost unbearable. The man taped her hands together behind her back, then pulled a small ball of rope from the shelf and stuffed it into his pocket. Lacey thought that, finally, the ordeal was over. He'd leave her there on the floor of the store. Soon she'd be able to go home to her babies and forget this had ever happened.

CHAPTER 4

Cody Lambert had graduated from Lakewood High the previous spring. He didn't have any aspirations of attending college, so he landed himself a good-paying job at a welding shop in Lakewood. The work was great and the pay consistent, which enabled him to get his own place – a small townhome with a garage and a fenced-in backyard.

As he always did, he woke up at four o'clock in the morning, then showered and dressed for the day. He drove to Joe's to get his morning cup of coffee, with hopes of chatting with Lacey, the pretty woman behind the counter. She talked about her kids with him. Cody assumed she was a little older than he was but he wasn't sure about women's ages. Cody had made it a habit to stop in every morning on his way to work. He looked forward to their talks but today was different. He was going to ask Lacey out. He knew that she might turn him down but he told himself that the risk far outweighed the gain. He couldn't hide his feelings for her anymore.

The door chime announced his entrance. He was excited to have finally built up the nerve to ask her out. But where was Lacey? He looked around. Usually, at this hour, she was behind the counter. When he looked over the counter, he saw that the cash register drawer was open. Only the change glimmered back at him. Turning quickly, he called out her name. No answer. Frantic, Cody ran down each aisle. He saw things tossed on the floor in the housewares section. When Lacey was there, she always picked up after messy customers and the store was always spotless.

He thought to himself, *Is it her day off?* No, it couldn't be. He poked his head into the back storage area and called out her name. Still no response. Cody rushed behind the counter and picked up the telephone.

"Nine-one-one, what's your emergency?" asked the Lakewood Police dispatcher.

"My name is Cody, Cody Lambert. I came into Joe's Convenience Store for a cup of coffee and no one is here. The ... cash register drawer is open but the lady who's always here is gone. There's no one here. Things are thrown on the floor. Something is wrong!"

"Sir, is there anyone in the store now?"

"No, that's why I'm calling you!"

"Sir, why don't you go out to your vehicle? Just stay there until I can get an officer out there," the dispatcher instructed.

Cody called work to tell them he'd be in late, and then returned to his truck. About ten minutes later, a uniformed officer arrived, followed by another officer. The Lakewood officer on the scene asked Cody what he had seen when he'd gotten to the store. By then, people were pulling up to the gas pumps, so another officer told them they would need to go elsewhere. Crime scene tape now roped off the pumps and the entrance to Joe's. Cody gave his statement to the uniformed officer, then was dismissed to go to his job. However, he found it hard to focus on his work, as he was worried about Lacey.

The owner of Joe's arrived and gave Lacey's emergency contact information to the officer. Lacey's brother was called and quickly arrived at Joe's. He asked the uniformed officer about her children, knowing that someone would need to pick them up.

Detective Connor Maxwell had been with the Lakewood Police Department for ten years. He had started as a uniformed patrolman and then worked his way up to the detective division. For the last five years, as the city of Lakewood grew, he had been teamed up with Detective Kate Stroup, who had done a lateral transfer to the division from the Boston Police Department. Connor and Kate were close in age. Both had been married once before and were now divorced. Their teamwork was impeccable. They also shared an attraction to each other. Connor and Kate made every effort to keep their relationship strictly business while on duty and to leave their work behind them when off duty. Nonetheless, Connor was finding it increasingly difficult. Before Kate, he had never seemed able to leave the job behind him when off duty. So, how could he be expected to do that now?

Kate had an athletic build. Her shoulder-length brown hair had natural red highlights. She looked like she should be walking the runway at some fashion show in New York City rather than carrying a Glock nine-millimeter pistol and a badge. She paddle-boarded in the summer, while in the winter she loved to mountain bike.

Connor was what some might call ruggedly handsome. His dark brown hair and dark brownish-green eyes attracted the opposite sex. He worked out at the Lakewood gym every day and had the physique to show for it. On his days off, he hiked the mountains around Lakewood with his canine companion, Sundae. Connor's wide shoulders and narrow waist made women turn whenever he walked into a room.

Kate opened the door to the small interview room. Connor was sitting across from Lacey's older brother.

"Sorry I'm late," Kate said as she glanced over at Connor and took the seat next to him. She could smell the light scent of Connor's shaving conditioner and she cleared her throat. "I'm Detective Kate Stroup," she said, extending her hand to the young man.

"Zackary Bryn," he said, taking her hand. "I'm Lacey's older brother. Please, call me Zack. As I was telling your partner, Lacey's children weren't picked up at the babysitter's that day. I know how it may look to some ... that she took the money and left. My sister wouldn't have left her kids…"

"Mr. Bryn."

"Call me Zack, please," he interrupted Kate. "Zack, we checked the activity on her debit card and nothing has been taken out. She's not answering her cell phone. Has your sister ever done this before? Just taken off for a few days?" asked Kate

Zack thought for a few minutes as the muscle in his jaw clenched. "No, not even as a teenager. But she would never have left her kids, never! Her ex-husband is a bum. He'd leave the kids but Lacey never would. Have you found Kyle yet? If he hurt her or had someone do something to her…"

"Zack, we're checking with his last employer. He was fired about two weeks ago."

"Figures," Zack said.

"As I was saying, he left no forwarding address. His latest girlfriend had kicked him out at about the same time. He's out there. I promise you, we'll find him," Kate said in a soft, calming voice.

"The blood that you found at the store. Was it hers?" Zack asked.

"We found her blood and an unidentified person's blood as well. She must have put up a fight. Thank you for the information on her car. We've already released that to law enforcement agencies across the country."

"This is Candy Martin with the five o'clock news. We'd like you to look at the photo on your screen now. If you have seen this woman, Lacey Warner, please call the hotline scrolling below."

The screen changed to a photo of Kyle. "Also, if you know the whereabouts of her ex-husband, Kyle Warner, we are told he is a person of interest. The Lakewood Police Department tells us that they simply need to talk to him."

Candy continued. "Lacey was believed to have been abducted from Joe's Convenience Store in the early morning hours. Police tell us there was a struggle. Lacey and her car, an older model Chevy Impala, were taken. FBI and local law enforcement have been working around the clock. FBI sources have told me that no ransom demand has been made."

CHAPTER 5

Connor Maxwell and Kate Stroup drove out to Joe's Convenience Store. The manager, a rotund man in his fifties, with a thick Middle Eastern accent, handed them a pink down-filled jacket belonging to Lacey.

"Is there anything else?" Connor asked

"Yes, a sweater." The manager hurried into the back and returned with a blue sweater, which, to Kate's eyes, looked to be a size small.

"You're sure this belonged to her?" Connor asked.

The man nodded.

"It's important," Connor said.

The owner looked down at the thirteen-inch beagle sitting next to Connor's left foot. "Yes ... yes, that belongs to Ms. Lacey," the owner said.

Connor and Kate thanked the manager and left.

As they drove north, Connor looked at the stretch of highway.

"So, the guy comes into the store. Why not fight? Why not toss cans of soup at the dude ... anything?" he mused out loud, tapping his thumbs on the steering wheel, deep in thought.

"Maybe he caught her by surprise. They found a carton of toilet paper that they thought she had been unpacking. Tossing rolls of TP wouldn't deter many people," Kate said.

Connor continued northbound out of Lakewood. "At that hour, no one's around. He abducts her. Where would he go?" Connor turned to glance at Kate, who was looking out the car window.

"We have no clue whether he's a local or a drifter just passing through town, so it's hard to say. Barton and Harris created a list of all the people in the area, both men and women, who have records and who are out on parole. Nothing." Kate brushed a lock of auburn hair behind one ear.

"The areas we've searched have all been in Lakewood and up to the Natick county line. They dredged the lake and the river. Nothing. If he took her out of the area..."

"Connor," Kate interrupted. "Every tip, every area we've searched, even if it's outside the Natick county line, has turned up nothing. No car, no trace of her. We have the State Police and the Sherriff's Department working the case alongside us."

CHAPTER 6

Connor stood beside his SUV and opened the rear door. Sundae, the thirteen-inch tri-colored beagle, jumped out and sat at Connor's left side. She looked up expectantly as Connor pulled out a bag and held Lacey's jacket up to Sundae's nose. It was his day off, but he felt a strong need to keep searching for Lacey.

Slowly, his thoughts drifted back to a case he had worked about a year ago—a young woman whose body was never found. Her father called every month, without fail, to ask if they knew anything about her whereabouts. Like other parents, the father wished, prayed, and hoped that if his loved one wasn't found, maybe she was still alive. Nonetheless, Connor also knew that finding the body allowed these parents to put closure to their heart-wrenching ordeal.

Each time, Connor found it harder to say no. The police department had no more leads, nor had they found the body. Connor never stopped looking; he was a cop who wouldn't quit. He told himself he owed that to these victims and their families. They were somebody's wife, husband, daughter, son, or another relative or friend. When the crime scene white board had been cleared off for the next case, Connor had taped the young woman's photo to his desk as a reminder to never give up the search.

Once again, he was searching for a young woman. They had tips and sightings but, so far, nothing had panned out. All they knew was that Lacey was a devoted mother of three who would never leave her young children behind. In his heart, her brother knew that her ex-husband had to be involved in her disappearance.

Connor cleared his thoughts and began walking the leaf-covered trail toward the mountains. Sundae ran in front of him. Connor had always loved hiking the mountain trails around Lakewood; he had done it as a boy and continued to do so as a man. Often, he would go up to the mountains simply to think. For hours, he would sit on a large rock overlooking the city below. This would allow him to distance himself and clear his mind as he tried to put together the puzzle pieces of the crime he was attempting to solve.

However, no matter how much he loved the mountains, he knew all too well that they were often a dumping ground and the resting place for bodies. Sundae sniffed and ran in her zigzag pattern, as she always did while searching. Connor scanned the trail ahead for anything that looked out of place. As he took off down a different trail, he could tell by the overgrowth that it was a less-traveled one. Nonetheless, he looked for freshly unearthed soil, a pile of brush that didn't belong...anything. He closed his eyes and silently prayed that Lacey wouldn't be another young woman whom he'd be searching for without answers for years.

Connor sat on a boulder and called Sundae over. He opened a collapsible bowl and pulled his water bottle from a holder on his belt. Then he poured Sundae a fresh bowl of water before taking a long pull from the bottle himself. Sundae sat beside him and he petted her, deep in thought.

His cell phone rang, startling him. "Maxwell," Connor said.

"Connor, I just got a lead," Kate said. "But before you get too excited, I should let you know that the uniforms tell me that the lady is very elderly...and her nickname is Sweeping Beauty."

"You mean Sleeping Beauty, right?"

"No, Sweeping Beauty. Seems she's out sweeping all hours of the day and night," Kate explained.

Connor and Kate sat in the living room of the small home furnished in mid-50s décor, including plastic covers on all the seats, mint green wallpaper dotted with small pink roses, and a colorful braided rug. Knick-knacks covered every inch of several shelves and an end table. Mrs. Kilgore carefully carried a tray of hot tea and cookies over to the coffee table. Connor watched her hand shake as she poured tea into each cup.

"I'm sorry I don't have anything for your little puppy," Mrs. Kilgore said, looking fondly at Sundae.

"That's okay, she really doesn't need any treats," Connor said with a smile.

"Mrs. Kilgore," Kate said. "When you called, you said you saw a man dragging a young woman away from the convenience store. That was about a week ago?"

"Oh, yes, dear. I did. I would have called again sooner had I known about the young lady being missing." Mrs. Kilgore took a sip from her teacup.

"Again?" Connor asked.

"My, yes, I called that morning. I was out on my porch sweeping off the leaves. I heard muffled screams and when I looked over, I saw a man dragging a young woman from the convenience store." She pointed in the general direction of Joe's Convenience Store.

Kate gave Connor a concerned look.

"Mrs. Kilgore, did an officer come over and talk to you about what you saw?" Connor asked.

"No." She shook her head. "No one came by at all."

"Do you remember if a patrol unit drove by the convenience store after your call to check it out?" asked Kate.

"I don't remember seeing one."

"We need to check and see who the uniform on duty was that morning," Connor told Kate as she quickly jotted down the information on her note pad.

"I guess no one takes an old lady very seriously," Mrs. Kilgore said, reaching for her teacup with a shaky hand.

"Mrs. Kilgore, I can assure you, we will look into this as soon as we get back to the police department," Kate said.

Connor pulled a photo out of the file. "Mrs. Kilgore, can you tell me if this woman looks like the young woman you saw being dragged out of the convenience store?"

Mrs. Kilgore held the photo in her hand and stared at the woman's picture. When she didn't say anything, Kate repeated the question. "Mrs. Kilgore, is this the same woman?"

"Can't be sure…my eyes aren't so good anymore at a distance, you know. But I think it looks like her.

Such a pretty young lady." Mrs. Kilgore handed back the photo.

"What about the man? Could you describe him to us?" Connor asked.

"He was taller than the woman..."

"Lacey Warner is five-foot-one. Knowing this, about how much taller was the man?" Kate asked.

"Oh, he was probably six feet. He has walked by my place a few times."

Connor leaned forward on the loveseat. "He has? Do you know what his name is, where he lives?"

"Why, no, he never talks. I've said hello a few times, but he never says a word. He smiled a few times. He's missing several teeth and the ones he has are yellow." She scrunched up her face. "Once, I was sweeping by my front fence and when he walked by, he had such an odor…like he hadn't bathed in days."

Kate wrote down everything that the woman said.

"Once, I shooed him off because he was at my gate, poking at my cat, Muffin, with a stick."

"And did he say anything to you or the cat then?" Connor asked.

"No, he just laughed at me."

"When he laughed, did he have a deep voice or a high-pitched voice?"

"Deep, a nasty laugh, like he enjoyed mistreating my cat."

"Mrs. Kilgore, would you mind if we sent a sketch artist over from the police department so you could describe the man to him?" Connor asked.

"Why no, not at all."

CHAPTER 7

Connor entered the police department dispatch area at the request of the dispatcher, who referenced a caller who would talk only to him.

"Did they say who's calling?"

"She refused to give me a name. Just said it's very important to the Lacey Warner case. She'll talk only to you," the dispatcher replied, looking up from her radio logs.

"Send the call to my phone," Connor said as he started back to his desk. He sat down and picked up on the first ring. "Maxwell. How can I help?"

"Connor, this is Sofie…" A soft voice trailed off.

Connor leaned back in his chair. He and Sofie had lived together years ago. He knew Sofie and Lacey had been best friends at Lakewood High. While Connor and Sofie were living together, Lacey had married Kyle Warner. Sofie had been the maid of honor at the wedding. Connor knew Lacey's abduction was probably weighing heavily on Sofie's heart. He could hear it in her voice.

"Do you have any information on the case?" Connor asked, trying to keep the call as professional as possible.

"Connor, first, I'm very sorry to bother you. I know…" Sofie's voice cracked as she fought off tears.

"What's the information, Sofie?" Connor said, not wanting to revisit their past.

Sofie hesitated. Clearly, Connor's short and to-the-point reply cut deeply.

"It's…Kyle. He's over at the Lakewood Bowling Alley."

"Is he there now?"

"Yes, he's sitting with a bunch of his buddies at the café."

"Sofie, thank you. I'll run by."

Connor disconnected the call. He grabbed his sport coat as Sundae followed closely behind him.

On the drive to the bowling alley, Connor wondered what Sofie was doing now. He knew she was trying very hard to become a pro bowler. They had been very young when they dated, and then they had drifted apart. Connor had moved on and that was the end of their story. But still, he wondered if he ever crossed her mind.

Kyle Warner sat nervously in what the Lakewood police officers called "the box." It was an interview room with three chairs, a camera, a recording device, a small table, and a one-way glass. Connor, Sundae, and Kate entered the room.

"Kyle, as you know already, my name is Detective Connor Maxwell. This is Detective Kate Stroup."

"And who's the mutt?" Kyle asked.

"The mutt, as you called her, is Lakewood's canine officer, Sundae."

Kyle chuckled at Kate's comment.

"Kyle, we will be recording this interview." Connor watched Kyle's body language. "Would you state your full name for the record?"

"Am I under arrest?" Kyle asked.

"Should you be?" Connor asked. Kyle said nothing. Connor continued to study him.

The answer came out grudgingly. "Kyle William Warner."

"Kyle, when your marriage to Lacey ended, would you say it was a mutual agreement between you and Lacey?" Kate asked.

"What?" Kyle said, with a smile on his face.

"Listen, punk," Connor said, standing up.

"Connor, let's talk outside," Kate said, trying to defuse the situation.

Frustrated, Connor stepped out into the hallway with Kate.

Kate reached over and straightened Connor's sport coat. "Why don't you let me talk to him?" She tilted her head to one side, looking at Connor.

"He's a jerk! Ex-wife or not, Lacey is the mother of his children and he doesn't seem to have any concern at all for what happened to her. Or his children."

"Wait here." Kate indicated the side of the glass where they were currently standing. She turned and walked back into the box.

Connor knew she was right. Already, he was losing his temper with Kyle. He knew Lacey and she'd disappeared on his watch. He wanted to bring her back alive, for her children...and, he had to admit, for Sofie as well.

He stood on the opposite side of the one-way glass and listened. As Kyle avoided answering questions, Kate continued pressing him. Finally, he asked for an attorney, which meant that Kate had to immediately stop the interview. She stepped out into the hallway and looked at Connor.

"I'm sorry, I tried," Kate said. She returned to the room and told Kyle he was free to go.

As Kyle stepped into the hallway, he grinned at Connor. "Detective," Kyle said, acknowledging him sarcastically, and then walked toward the exit.

He never it made it through the doorway. Two uniformed officers took hold of him.

"What? Listen, I know my rights. I asked for an attorney!" Kyle tried to pull away.

Kyle Warner, you're under arrest for back child support."

"Did you...?" Kate looked at Connor.

"I'll never tell," Connor said as he turned and walked in the opposite direction, with Sundae following on his heels.

As Connor stepped into the lobby, Sofie ran to him and flung her arms around him, crying. Kate stopped just before the door closed.

"Connor, I'm so sorry. I know I shouldn't have come down here. Does he have Lacey? Does he know where she is?

Connor pulled away from her embrace and handed his handkerchief to her. She dabbed at her eyes.

"Sofie, he lawyered up."

"He what?"

"He requested an attorney."

"And?"

"We can no longer talk to him without his attorney present."

"Kyle is a deadbeat. The man doesn't even have an attorney," Sofie blurted out in frustration.

"Sofie, the state will appoint one for him."

"So, he just gets to walk out of here while Lacey is…God knows where."

"Sofie, I had him placed under arrest for back child support. Lacey's brother told us he's never paid her a dime in child support. We can't hold him very long but at least we have him for now."

Connor looked behind him for Kate and saw a closed door.

"Listen, Sofie, I'm really sorry about Lacey. We're doing everything we can to find her."

Sofie reach over and hugged Connor. "Thank you. I miss you." Sofie leaned back and looked at Connor. "I don't miss what you do for a living. Every time I hear that a cop has been…" Sofie's sentence trailed off.

"Sof, listen. I promise you that if we find her, I'll let you know," Connor said.

She turned and walked away.

CHAPTER 8

Connor stared at the white board; it was bare in comparison to other crimes they had worked in the past.

"What are we missing?" Connor asked himself in frustration.

Kate looked up from a report she was working on and watched him pace like a nervous cat in front of the white board. Kate had been exceptionally quiet since she'd seen Sofie and Connor's interaction the other day. She found herself wondering whether Connor still had feelings for the woman...or was what he said really true—that their relationship was truly in the past?

"For one thing, we don't have Lacey or the ID of the person who dragged her away from the store. Her car is still missing," Kate offered.

Connor flopped down in his desk chair and

leaned his head back. He looked upward and closed his eyes, as if the answers he so desperately needed would somehow come from the heavens above.

Kate's desk phone rang. "Detective Stroup."

Connor tried to block out the one-way conversation that was going on across from him at Kate's desk. Kate hung up the phone and quickly opened her email on her computer. She stared at the image on her screen, then hit the print icon. She grabbed the artist sketch from the printer and taped it to the white board across from Lacey's photo. With a dry erase marker, she drew a line from Lacey's photo to the sketch.

"We have this!" Kate said.

Connor opened his eyes. In one fluid motion, he turned, glanced at the photo, lifted himself out of his chair, and walked over to the white board where Kate had taped the pencil sketch of a man.

"Sweeping Beauty"—Mrs. Kilgore—had helped the police sketch artist render a drawing of the man whom she had seen that night and who would walk by her house on occasion. Connor walked closer to the board, studying the sketch. His eyes were pulled toward the missing teeth. The sketch didn't look anything like Kyle Warner, and Kyle had no missing teeth—at least not now. Connor had his doubts as to whether Lacey's brother would be able to control himself if he and Kyle crossed paths.

"We need this sent to the media, all law enforcement agencies, and everyone we can," Connor said. "I'm going down to the first floor to give a copy to the uniforms." He reached for his sport coat.

"Connor." Kate grabbed for his arm to pull him back. "I've already given it to Sandy in dispatch and asked her to make sure all patrol units have it, as well as the media outlets and outside law enforcement agencies. We have something else. Come with me."

Connor and Sundae followed Kate to the elevator and down to the first-floor police lab.

Connor stood before a steel table where a shoe cast lay.

"Remember that Mrs. Kilgore told us the man she saw drag Lacey from the store had walked by?" Kate asked. "She remembered that it had rained the day before and that his shoe print was still there, outside her fence. CSI went out after Mrs. Kilgore showed it to the sketch artist."

The lab tech said, "What we have here is a man's Nike size-12 cross trainer. While they make thousands of this type of shoe, see this?" He used his pencil to direct their attention to a large cut on the heel. "While thousands of size-12 shoes of this very type may exist, only one right shoe will have this cut on the heel."

Within the hour, Connor, Kate, and Sundae were back at Mrs. Kilgore's house. Connor looked at the footprint that matched the print back at the Lakewood police lab. The tech had taken a photo of the cast, so Connor compared it to the imprints in the soil. Sure enough, in each step this person had taken, the right shoe showed the line, or cut, as the tech had described it. Just as Mrs. Kilgore had stated, the unknown man had walked northbound from her home.

Sundae sniffed the footprints in the dried soil but Connor doubted that there was any scent the little beagle would be able to track. It had been raining, plus several days had passed since the footprints had been left in the soil. Nevertheless, the three followed the footprints north from Mrs. Kilgore's house until they ended at a gas station's concrete driveway. Connor went to the other side of the driveway, where he could see that the prints continued until the dirt pathway gave way to dense grass. There, the tracks disappeared. Connor stopped. He looked to the north, then back at Kate.

"We're within a few hundred yards of the Indian reservation," Connor said.

"Does that mean you think he lives on the reservation?"

"I hope not. That would open a whole new can of worms," Connor said, a concerned look on his face.

Just then, Sundae darted across Main Street

toward a trailer park located just inside the Lakewood city limits. Connor and Kate followed. The little beagle kept her nose to the ground the whole way. Once across the street, Sundae ran from one trailer house to the next, up on each trailer's porch and then down again.

"I wish we had Lacey's jacket with us," Connor said.

Kate offered to run back to their unit to get it.

"While you do that, I'll follow Sundae," Connor said.

Once Kate had headed back to the car, Connor picked up his cell phone and dialed an old friend. His name was Alex Yazzie, a Navajo Indian who had worked for, and retired from, the FBI years ago. When Connor had first started as a uniformed officer, he had watched Yazzie track a man wanted for murder. The other agents could never figure out how Yazzie could create a profile of a subject by the tracks the person left behind. To Yazzie, this was second nature, a skill passed down from generation to generation of Navajos. He had tried many times to pass the skill along to Connor.

About the same time, Kate pulled up and retrieved the jacket from the bag in the truck. Alex pulled his Jeep alongside their car, which was a plain-vanilla sedan, otherwise known as an unmarked car. When she saw Alex, Kate smiled and gave him a big hug.

"Kate, you're prettier every time I see you." Alex looked Kate over. "Hope this white man knows how lucky he is to have a partner like you."

Kate blushed at the comment.

"What do you have?" Alex asked, changing the subject.

Connor pulled the photo from his sport coat pocket and showed the footprint cast to Alex. Alex put the heel of his boot on one of the Jeep's tires and leaned forward to support his weight as he studied the photo.

"This is from a male. I'm sure you both already know that," Alex said. "Do we have any tracks around here that I can see?"

"We followed them up to the grass across the street," Connor said.

"Take me," Alex said.

Connor, Kate, and Sundae took Alex back to the last set of tracks. Alex crouched down and studied the tracks. After five minutes, Kate wondered what Alex could be looking at for so long. After ten minutes, Alex looked up at Connor.

"Were you able to get anything from these?" Alex asked.

"Didn't really have a chance."

Alex shook his head and smiled. "Well, the person who left these is left-handed."

Connor bent down and studied the tracks. Alex stood up beside Kate.

"He's left-handed…by the weight on the left foot print?" Connor looked up at Alex.

"Now there is something else I noticed," Alex said. He pointed at the trail of tracks behind them. "Notice the steps he takes aren't uniform at all. There's no debris on the trail, at least not at this time, to account for a person doing that. This person is what we Navajos would call *T'oo diigis*. In white man's terms, a crazy man."

"Could he have been drunk?" Kate asked.

Alex looked over at her. "No."

CHAPTER 9

Sundae never took her eyes off of Main Street as Alex said his goodbyes and began to cross the highway to where he had parked. The beagle ran past Alex as he opened the door to his Jeep. She continued on toward a small white and blue trailer house. Connor and Kate called Sundae, who was barking at the underside of the trailer. Connor walked across the street to where Sundae was crouched down and barking frantically.

As Connor approached her, a powder-gray and white cat burst out from under the house.

"Sundae, you know better than that. A cat, *really?*" Connor said, taking hold of her collar.

Just then, his cell phone rang. "Maxwell," Connor said.

"Natick County just recovered Lacey's car," the Lakewood Police Department dispatcher said.

"Was she in it?

"Negative. But County wants our CSI team there. I've already dispatched them and I'm sending the location to your phones," Sandy said.

While Connor was on the phone with dispatch, Sundae had managed to run back to the same trailer house. She began barking again. Connor quickly gathered her up under his arm. As soon as he placed Sundae in the back seat, he told Kate that County had located Lacey's car and that Sandy was sending the location to their phones.

As Connor pulled his unmarked unit around, Sundae stood on the arm rest and barked in the direction of the white and blue trailer house.

Connor, Kate, and Sundae walked toward the old blue Chevy Impala. Natick County Sheriff's Deputy Jamie Kraft walked toward Kate and Connor.

"Looks like it was run until it ran out of gas. There are tracks leading back this way." Jamie pointed toward the highway. "There's some blood in the back seat. Looks like the young lady put up a fight."

Connor walked over to Sundae and gave her a release command. He put on his latex gloves and then looked into the car. There, he saw a Styrofoam coffee cup in a cup holder and a receipt from a store.

Connor looked at the trunk, which was already open. It contained a car seat and some children's clothes but nothing else. Connor walked back to his unit and popped open the trunk. He held Lacey's coat to Sundae's nose. "Find Lacey," he commanded.

Sundae ran her zigzag pattern back and forth.

"You stay here with the CSI team while they process the car. I'll go with Sundae and see if she finds anything," Connor said as he passed Kate.

Connor looked at the tracks leading away from the Chevy. The imprint of the shoes matched the prints from the front of Mrs. Kilgore's home. This confirmed to Connor that the man who had walked by Mrs. Kilgore's house was the same male suspect who had pulled Lacey into her car.

However, this time he noticed the overall pattern of the tracks in the soil. Once again, there was no debris in the trail but a staggered walking pattern led toward the highway. It was the same manner of walking that Alex had picked up on.

Once at the highway, Connor called Sundae into the deep brush as they looked for clues. After nearly two hours of searching, Connor and Sundae came back full circle to the Chevy Impala, just as the wrecker was loading it onto a rollback truck.

"Anything?" Kate asked.

"Nothing. We went to the highway and then circled all the way around this area. Not a damn thing."

"The CSI team was able to lift some prints off the dash," Kate said. "But the steering wheel seems to have been wiped clean—or, Chris said, if the suspect had worn a pair of cloth gloves, it would make it look like the steering wheel had been wiped clean. As he turned the steering wheel, it would have slid through his gloved hands."

There was blood and some long hair on the backseat. They also found some rope.

They'll be able to pull DNA off the coffee cup. Connor, this doesn't look good for Lacey."

Connor looked down at his dusty boots, thinking.

"If Lacey was alive, he couldn't very well have waltzed her out to the highway and walked somewhere. There was only one set of tracks and that matched the ones in front of Mrs. Kilgore's house. Also, the imprint in the soil tells me he wasn't carrying anything like a person," Connor said, looking up at Kate.

"So, she's either someplace he left her while he disposed of the car or she's…"

"Dead." Connor finished her sentence.

"Let's hope, for the children's sake, it's not the latter," Kate said as the three of them got into the police unit.

Several days after Lacey's abduction, he walked into the bar across from Joe's Convenience Store. After several beers, he paid his tab and then walked over to the post office lobby. The pretty little red-haired girl wasn't there anymore. This was the third time he'd walked to the bar to get a drink and watch TV and she wasn't there anymore. It was about one in the morning as he stood in the dimly lit lobby, watching two workers restock the shelves. Only now there was one male and one female employee. He left the post office and walked north toward his house.

Mrs. Kilgore had been sweeping her front porch. As she always did, she stopped when she thought she heard someone talking. Quickly and quietly, she ceased sweeping and sat on her porch swing, still clutching her broom. She could make out a shadow approaching from the south, walking northward.

Was it him—that big man who had dragged the poor, helpless woman from Joe's Convenience Store? Hadn't the police found him yet? Maybe they had and it wasn't the man they were looking for. Mrs. Kilgore wondered if she should have gotten her cordless phone, just in case, but the phone was inside and she was out on the porch. His mumbling was louder now as he neared her property line and passed her mailbox. Mrs. Kilgore leaned forward. As she did, the porch swing's chains made an audible creek.

CHAPTER 10

*E*dward A. Bolton sat back, enjoying his morning coffee in his heated sunroom. As he took a sip, he looked over his lavish yard and the stonework he had paid handsomely for last summer. The sprawling 15-acre estate had been in his family for over a hundred years. It featured a luxurious 5,000-square-foot home and a 1,300-square-foot guesthouse equipped with a kitchen and laundry. The servants' quarters were an additional 1,200 square feet. There was also a detached five-car garage and a rose garden.

Ed picked up his cell phone and clicked on the speed dial for his son. The phone rang, but only reached a digitized voice instructing the caller to leave a message.

"Damn it!" Mr. Bolton swore, looking at the phone. Twelve calls had been made to this number in the last week with no answer. 'You'd better not have gotten yourself into any trouble,' Bolton thought to himself. His mind ran through several different scenarios involving things his son could have gotten involved in again.

He stood at the foot of his bed, looking at his prize, the young woman he had taken against her will and brought to his home. She was a fighter, that was for sure. Even with her hands secured behind her back, she had managed to kick him several times—once between the legs before she had started to run. He had caught her and, in an angry fit, hit her several times in the face until she lay unconscious at his feet. He smiled now, knowing that, with her tied to his bed and a gag in her month, he was in control.

She was asleep. Her face was badly bruised and dried blood was caked on her bottom lip. He remembered that he had bitten her bottom lip last night. He'd removed the gag from her month and tried to kiss her, the way he'd seen it done in his movies. But she'd told him his breath stank and he stank. He'd slapped her and stuck the gag back in her mouth.

The bedroom reeked, as he refused to untie the woman to allow her to use the restroom. She had no alternative other than to relieve herself on his bed.

He would give her water when she asked. She refused any food he tried to give to her, saying his hands were filthy. She didn't want anything those hands had touched.

She wasn't as pretty anymore, he thought to himself, with her hair all matted and uncombed, and her face so swollen. What should he do with her? He could kill her and put her in the trashcan. Trash pickup was tomorrow, wasn't it? Or was that yesterday? If only he still had her car, but it had stopped running. He'd left it, as it had ceased to be of use to him. Much like she was to him right now.

He turned, walked back into the living room of the old house, and grabbed the cable TV remote. He flipped through the channels until he found just what he was looking for. His therapist back in Boston had told him that he had an addiction to porn. She told him to never again watch it after he had been taken to the mental hospital. There, he could not watch any TV like that, not like his all-day binge watching in his bedroom while his father was at work. What did that old lady in Boston know, anyway? She was old and wrinkled, and she wore high-neck blouses and long skirts.

Lacey lay there and dreamed that she was free—free of this madman and free of this room with its overwhelming stench. She dreamed of her three children playing out front on the lawn. When the TV woke her up, she wanted to scream but he had put a wash towel in her mouth and duct-taped over it. She wondered where she was. Could no one hear her? Come to her rescue? She was unconscious when he'd dragged her into this room. How many days had she been there? She tried to remember. Was it two, three…a week? Was anyone looking for her?

Lacey raised her head from the pillow. She was weak, refusing food and taking only water from the man when he offered it. She looked around with her good eye. The other one was swollen shut. The windows were darkened with something more than just curtains, so it was impossible to tell how many days or nights had passed. It was just one long, dark night that lasted forever. She could hear the front door open and close when he left the house. At those times, she tried to pull her hands and legs free but to no avail. Several times, he had turned on the bedroom light and stood at the foot of the bed, looking at her. During one of those times, she had peeked and seen the rope that he had taken from Joe's—the one that bound her hands.

She knew he hadn't taken a shower since she had woken up. The first time he'd laid down on the bed with her, she thought she would vomit from the smell. How could he live like this? For that matter, how could he do the things he had been doing to her? There had to be a way out of this house and away from him. She had no idea where her clothes were, but, if given the chance to get loose, she would run with or without clothes for help. She had never hated anyone in her life, not even Kyle, but she hated this monster of a man.

Lacey heard his groaning as the TV was turned off. Footsteps came down the hallway, approaching the door. Quickly, Lacey shut her eyes and pretended to be asleep. 'Not again, please, God, not again,' she thought as she felt his weight on the bed and his hands on her body.

CHAPTER 11

Deep in thought, Connor took a long pull from his beer. Today had been just another day spent chasing tips with the same result. Nothing.

Kate studied him from across the small wooden table. "Something is eating at you. Want to talk about it?" she asked.

Connor looked around the local bar and grill. Then he spoke up. "I'm tired of letting families down. They need to have answers ... answers I can't find, bodies I can't find." He leaned back in the chair and closed his eyes.

Kate could see that Connor was struggling, as so many detectives did when sensing a case growing colder by the day. The fact was, this case had seemed cold shortly after Lacey's abduction, she thought to herself.

"Connor, I know it's hard, but they teach us all at the academy, detach yourself." Kate paused, then finished. "Or you'll drive yourself crazy."

"I try but…"

"Connor, you still have Mia Gordon's photo on your desk. How many months has that been? I know you go out hiking and are still looking for her. You mentioned something about it a while back to Sandy in dispatch. You're letting this stuff eat you up inside."

Connor looked away. He knew Kate was right but he hated leaving things unfinished. It was just something that was ingrained in him and couldn't be changed, much like his DNA. Even as a child, he would finish one lesson in school before moving on to the next. *Focus and finish*, his mom would say. That's what he'd done until he joined the police department. All too often, all the focus in the world couldn't help him, or any detective, stamp the word "closed" on a case.

"If I don't keep looking, who will?" Connor asked as he peeled the label off the beer bottle in front of him.

"Connor, we can only work with the facts we have. In this case, there's very little to go on. Hell, if that uniformed patrolman would have done his job and followed up with Mrs. Kilgore's call, and then gone to Joe's that morning, we'd have been hours ahead of the curve," Kate said.

Connor ran his hand through his hair.

Kate threw a few questions at him. "What if Mrs. Kilgore is just what the uniform said? A lonely old lady who just wanted company? What if it was Kyle, her ex-husband? What if Lacey had enough of being a single parent and took the money and ran? What if Cody, who called her disappearance into the PD, is the person we should be looking at?"

"Kate, we know that the shoeprint matches the one Mrs. Kilgore showed to the police and the one found leading away from Lacey's car. As for Cody, he admitted that he wanted to ask Lacey out, so, sure, she could have turned him down that morning. His ego couldn't take it and things got out of hand. We can bring him back in for questioning. As for Kyle, honestly, if it doesn't involve a party, booze, getting laid, or girls, I don't see it happening."

He continued. "Lacey took care of those three kids and Kyle never visited them or paid a dime in support. My gut feeling is that he forgot her and the kids the day he closed the front door and walked out on them. And as for Lacey not wanting to be a single parent and leaving her three children, I may be wrong, but everyone we talked to says she would never leave those kids."

"Everyone ... like Sofie?" The words slipped out of Kate's mouth before she could stop them.

Connor looked up at her. "Seriously? Are you jealous of Sofie? Is that what this is all about?"

Kate said nothing. She knew what she'd said was wrong. There was no retracting the words, no do-overs. The question lingered in the air between them like a bad odor.

"Okay ... I guess I was a little concerned when she hugged you the other day, but..."

Connor interrupted her. "Sofie and I are in the past. She hated me being a cop."

"But what about you? Do you still love her?"

"Kate, I did for a while after we broke up ... but I had to realize that my profession and Sofie didn't work together. We tried. I said I'd quit. I even typed up my resignation but never turned it in. Once Sofie saw that, we were finished. We were young and maybe I didn't love her like I should have."

Kate felt foolish, acting like a jealous high schooler. It was clear that there had once been deep feelings, but she believed Connor. What was on Sofie's mind was another issue, but Kate knew Connor well enough to realize that if he said it was over, then it was.

"Why don't we bring Cody in one more time, have another look at him? I know the sketch doesn't match, nor does the shoe size, but maybe two people were working together in her abduction," Kate said, changing the subject.

"Why don't we bring in Beth Ellis?" Connor asked. Beth was a psychologist who had worked with the FBI Behavior Science Division, as well as on previous cases with Connor and other law enforcement agencies across the country.

"On the case in general or just this interview with Cody?" asked Kate.

"Let's bring her in on the case. I know we don't have a lot of info for her, but maybe she'll see something we missed. In the morning, I'll email her and send over what we have." Connor stood, pulled a twenty from his wallet, and tossed it on the table for their tab and a tip.

Kate pushed back her chair. "Connor, I'm sorry about the Sofie thing. Really."

"I better get home," Connor said, looking at his watch. "Sundae's dinner will be late and she's probably pacing the house, wondering where I am."

He sat at the bar in the old dive, watching TV and finishing his beer. That pretty news reporter lady came on the screen. She reported that, according to the Lakewood Police, there was a person of interest in the Lacey Warner case. A police sketch artist's rendering of a man filled the screen.

"The man whom Lakewood Police want to talk to has no front teeth and wears a size 12 Nike shoe like this." The camera panned back to Candy Martin as she held up the shoe to show viewers at home. "If you know this man or have seen him, please call the number at the bottom of your TV screen."

Quickly, he looked down and away from the TV on the wall and smiled into the smoky mirror. The sketch looked just like him. Then he looked down at his shoes. It was that girl's fault, he mumbled to himself. It was all her fault, this whole thing! Quickly, he paid his tab and left the bar.

That night, he didn't go into the old post office lobby to watch the employees at Joe's and re-live the early morning he'd abducted her. Instead, he headed north, all the while talking to himself.

"Bitch, that bitch, it's all her fault!"

Mrs. Kilgore heard him before she saw the shadow of the man approaching her yard. 'Is it him?' she wondered as she quickly entered her front door and locked it behind her. She grabbed her phone and called the Lakewood Police Department.

He heard the front door shut just as he opened the front gate and walked onto the porch. He put his hand on the doorknob but it was locked. Mrs. Kilgore watched from the darkened kitchen. In the moonlight, she saw the doorknob turn left and right, but the door didn't open. She breathed a sigh of relief.

"Lakewood Police Department, what's your emergency?"

"Bitch, I know you're in there!"

Mrs. Kilgore slowly moved to the hallway and

grabbed her broom with one hand, while holding the phone in the other. She heard the front window, next to the door, being pushed upward. She thought that surely the shadowy figure must hear her heart beating. The window edged up slowly, the years of paint keeping it from opening faster. Then she saw his large, dirty hand reach under the frame and tug.

"Lakewood Police Department, what's your emergency?" Sandy repeated to the caller.

CHAPTER 12

Mrs. Kilgore heard the man pushing the window upward. As he gave one last tug, the paint gave way. Mrs. Kilgore opened the hall closet slowly, entered with her broom, and quietly closed the door behind her.

"Hurry, PLEASE. He got the window up," she said in a low voice.

"Stay on the phone. Don't hang up. The officer is about three minutes away," the Lakewood dispatcher said.

The man leaned back, still holding on to the window frame, trying to put his leg inside the house through the open window. At the same moment, Mrs. Kilgore's cat, Muffin, sprang through the window. The cat connected with the man's face, scaring both of them. Grabbing at his face, the man let go of the window frame and rolled backward onto the front porch. Muffin let go with a cry and ran off the front porch. The cat turned and looked at the man as he got up, then ran under a bush. Hearing the sirens approach, the man ran and hid just as a police car turned the corner at the end of the street.

Connor sighed heavily as he sat behind the wheel. When he inserted the ignition key, he heard a radio transmission from the Lakewood Police dispatcher, requesting a uniformed unit at 1312 Oak Street for a home invasion in progress. Connor thought the address sounded familiar, then dismissed it, thinking of the many addresses he'd been to in the last few weeks alone. Flipping on the headlights, he turned out of the driveway and headed for home. Suddenly, it hit him. He swerved into the oncoming lane of traffic, making a U-turn.

"15, PD is that Mrs. Kilgore's house?" Connor asked.

"10-4."

"15, PD, show me en route."

Connor stepped on the gas. Kate heard the radio transmission and also headed to Mrs. Kilgore's house. "49, PD, en route as well," she said.

The home was dark when Connor pulled up two houses away from Mrs. Kilgore's. The street was dark, lit only by a single streetlight at the end of the road. Kate, with her headlights out, pressed her mic button twice, signaling Connor that she was there and approaching from the other direction. Connor noticed Kate pulling up to the curb and motioned for her to approach from that side of the street.

When he got out of his unit, he saw no sign of Mrs. Kilgore or the uniformed officer. As Connor approached the house, he heard a sound coming from the backyard. Slowly, he walked to the back, his gun drawn. The amber glow from the single streetlight cast long shadows from the overgrown bushes and trees, creating an eerie look.

As Connor approached an overgrown evergreen bush, something burst out from under the brush in front of him. Connor crouched in a firing stance and took aim before realizing that it was Mrs. Kilgore's cat.

'Damn you, Peaches, Cookie, Muffin, whatever the hell your name is!' he thought to himself, his heart still pounding. "What are you doing out at night?"

He remembered that Mrs. Kilgore had told them that she never let out the cat without her. Was Mrs. Kilgore in the back yard? Had the home invader let out the cat? Connor had no idea. Slowly, he walked to the southernmost corner of the yard. His eyes were drawn to what looked like a flashlight on the opposite side of the fence. Carefully, he glanced over and saw the uniformed officer cuffing a man in boxer shorts. The officer pulled the man to his feet.

"Detective Maxwell," Connor called out to the officer from his side of the fence as he holstered his weapon and climbed over into the yard behind Mrs. Kilgore's.

"I'm telling you the truth … I heard a noise out back. This is my house and I came out to check it out, that's all."

As Connor neared him, he saw that the boxer-clad man was Cody Lambert.

"Have you made contact with the caller?" Connor asked the uniformed officer.

"PD has her on the phone. She's hiding in a hallway closet with dispatch still on the line."

"I'll take him in for questioning while you take the report from the caller," Connor said, taking Cody by the shoulder.

"Questioning? I was only checking out a noise I heard. That's all!" Cody pleaded.

Cody sat in the wooden chair, dressed in an orange inmate jumpsuit that Connor had given him to wear Kate and Connor looked in from the one-way glass in the hallway.

"From what Garcia said, after he took Mrs. Kilgore's statement, the man attempted to get in through the front window once he found her front door locked. He kept saying, 'Bitch, you're to blame,' over and over again. I guess Mrs. Kilgore assumes someone from our department leaked her name and address. She believes the man came after her," Kate said.

Connor thought for a minute. "A leak from our department?"

"Only repeating what Garcia told me."

Connor opened the door to the interview room. He and Kate took their seats.

"Cody, as you as you know, we videotape and record everything that goes on in this room," Connor said.

Cody nodded.

Connor continued. "Cody, please state your full name for the record."

After several hours of questioning, a very scared Cody was released after agreeing to allow a CIS team to examine his house and cell phone records.

Connor knew they had nothing concrete to hold him on, so he had a patrol unit take Cody back to his house. In addition, Connor instructed the CIS team to try lifting prints from Mrs. Kilgore's front doorknob and window. He also requested that the desk sergeant have patrol units go by Mrs. Kilgore's house day and night several times for her protection.

The next day, Connor sent an email to Beth Ellis, asking if she had time to look over the Warner case. She agreed and Kate took a copy of the file over to her office. After Mrs. Kilgore's fear of a leak, Connor kept the original file with him in the car.

The following day, Connor picked up Carlos, a young boy whom he and Kate had met during another, earlier case. Carlos lived with only his grandmother, so Connor had taken the boy under his wing. He made it a point of finding time to do things with Carlos and his dog. After meeting Sundae, Carlos had really wanted to keep her, which, of course, wasn't possible. Eventually, Connor found a little beagle for the young boy, who named the dog Pebbles. Connor had paid for Pebbles' training, first in obedience and currently in a tracking program.

Connor headed over to Mrs. Kilgore's house with Carlos and the two beagles. He took Sundae and Pebbles up on the porch, where Sundae immediately picked up a scent. With her nose to the ground, she ran to the neighbor's yard and disappeared into a large bush bordering the two properties. Pebbles followed Sundae. It was clear to Connor that Pebbles was unsure of what was going on, as she ran back to Carlos. Several seconds later, Sundae rushed out of the bush with her nose to the ground and her tail up in her zig-zag search pattern. She headed north from Mrs. Kilgore's house. Connor, Carlos, and Pebbles continued to follow Sundae. She stopped where she had paused the other day, where the tall grass covered the path near the reservation. This time, she looked up at Connor. The traffic was much heavier today compared to the other day, so Connor walked her across the street, where she resumed her searching pattern. Once more, she stopped, sat, and barked at the old blue and white trailer.

Connor stepped onto the front porch, which was badly in need of repair, and knocked on the front door. There was no answer. He walked around the mobile home, trying to look in, but the windows were covered in aluminum foil. He went to the back door and knocked but no one answered. Connor wrote the address on the palm of his hand. Before leaving, he knocked and called out at the front door. Still, there was no answer.

When Connor turned to leave, he didn't see the finger peeling an edge of the aluminum foil away from one of the mobile home's windows. Once Connor was back in the car, he called dispatch and asked if they could look up property records to find out who owned 24 Trixie Lane, Space B.

CHAPTER 13

The telephone sat on an old, secondhand oak kitchen table that had come with the house. It began to ring and he pushed aside several stacks of X-rated magazines. Finding the phone, he saw the caller ID and let the phone continue to ring. He stood up and pushed the curtains to one side, then peeled back a corner of the aluminum foil that he had placed on the windows. He glanced out, then put the foil back. Having seen no one around, he left through the front door and locked it behind him.

He walked to the old dive and let his eyes adjust as he stepped inside. Then he ordered a beer. At this hour, the place was almost empty, except for a young man nursing a beer at the opposite side of the bar. He finished and paid his bill.

When he walked outside, the sunlight almost blinded him. He looked over the parking lot. Only one of the parking slots was taken, occupied by a new-model pickup truck. He thought that it probably belonged to the young man inside, drowning his sorrows in his beer.

Lacey heard the front door open and close. She heard the TV turn on. He was home again. She dreaded him. It was always the same—he left, came back, and then the porn came on. She was weak from not eating. He gave her water but not consistently enough to keep her hydrated. She had refused food the first few days, as his hands were as filthy as his body. As the days went by, the hunger pangs became terrible and she would have taken something, anything to eat. But after she had refused a few times, he no longer offered her food. He reminded her of a child who had to be reminded to feed and water his pet. Only no one was there to remind him to feed and water her.

She looked at the overhead light as the room begin to spin. Her lips were so dry and cracked and her body itched from head to toe. Was it from dehydration? Or was it because she wasn't able to wash herself properly? Or was her body shutting down, organ by organ?

At this point, her mind was foggy and kept repeating the same questions over and over, like a broken record. On several occasions, she'd begun to hallucinate about being home in her own bed, listening for the children to come bounding down the hallway, jump in bed with her, and tell her, "Mommy, let's do breakfast." But there were no children—only a beast of a man holding her against her will.

The gag—stuffed in her mouth to prevent her from screaming—only worsened the dryness in her mouth. When would this nightmare end? The last time he was with her, she'd pleaded with him to either give her water or end her life and suffering.

Then, like always, she heard his heavy footsteps coming down the hallway. She felt his weight on the side of the bed and his rough, filthy hands touch her. How could she endure another time with this animal? Why was this happening to her? Keeping her good eye closed, she pretended to be asleep and prayed that he would leave her alone. But he didn't. After he was finished with her, he dressed himself, then untied her wrists and ankles.

"Get up," he demanded in a gruff voice.

She tried to sit up but didn't have the strength. On her failed third attempt, he grabbed her left arm and jerked her to her feet. She was dizzy and started to faint. He sat her on the edge of the bed and wrapped her in the filthy bed sheet on which she'd laid. Then he tossed her over his shoulder and carried her down the long walkway. She blacked out several times. When she came to, she tried to focus her eyes but everything was a blur.

The next time she woke up, they were in a truck, not her car. Where was her car? She would need it to get to and from work. This was a new truck. Where were they? Where was he taking her? Why did the bright sunlight hurt her eyes so badly?

"Water, please," she pleaded with him.

"I don't have any water!" he yelled.

"Please, just some water. That's all I ask."

He pulled off I-25, heading east across the mesa toward an arroyo. There, he stopped the truck. Then he got out and looked at the dry arroyo bed. The previous rainfall had littered it with people's discarded trash, which had rushed down through the arroyo until the water had stopped flowing. He turned and saw her slumped to one side on the truck seat.

He contemplated what to do with her. He could leave her in the truck, as she was too weak to get help. He could pull her out and dump her into the arroyo. In her condition, she'd never be able to get herself out. He guessed the dirt walls of the arroyo were fifteen to twenty feet high. But what if someone found her and she could talk? What if he had to go to jail?

He walked back to the truck, then opened the door and, with a harsh jerk, pulled her out. Her bare ankle caught on the seat, leaving a gash that spilled blood onto the floormat. He forced her to the edge of the arroyo. She was facing him, not knowing how perilously close she was to the edge.

"No, please, don't hurt me!" she pleaded, looking him straight in the eyes as he supported her weak body.

Swiftly, without any emotion or concern for her wellbeing, he thrust her body backward over the edge and watched her tumble down the wall of the arroyo.

Her mind thought that she and the children were at the Lakewood Park, rolling down the big grassy hill. She heard their laugher and saw their smiling faces. Then her head hit a rock protruding from the face of the arroyo.

Her body rolled another five feet and hit another rock before coming to rest at the bottom of the arroyo. He stood there smiling until he noticed her trying to lift her head. This angered him. Quickly, he ran down into the arroyo and toward her body.

He drove through town and pulled into a self-service car wash. Once inside, he opened all the doors, inserted several quarters, and flipped the dial settings to soap. He sprayed the truck's interior until the seats, dashboard, door handles, and windshield were covered in suds. Then he flipped it to rinse and repeated the process. After that, he washed the outside of the truck. Once he was done, he looked around. Satisfied that no one was watching, he walked away, leaving the truck inside one of the wash bays.

CHAPTER 14

The terminal was crowded at this late hour. He clutched the ticket he had purchased, waiting for his departure time. As a line of people formed under the sign that read Denver, he picked up his bag and followed the other passengers waiting to board.

It was Saturday and the car wash bays were beginning to fill up. Richard Dunkin had started working at the car wash a week ago. He was still learning the customers' needs, the machines, and the quirks of all the equipment. Like this vacuum that was taking people's money but refusing to turn on even after it was fed the correct number of quarters.

"Hey, kid," called out a man from the open window of his shiny red Camaro.

Richard looked up and walked toward him. "Yes, sir, what can I help you with?"

"That truck over there," the man pointed to the end bay, "it's been here since early this morning. I washed my car and now my wife's and it hasn't moved."

Richard looked over to where the man was pointing. "Thank you," he replied as the man pulled the Camaro out of the driveway.

He walked over to what looked like a brand-new three-quarter-ton Ford truck. Richard couldn't help but notice all the chrome trim, from the running boards to the bumpers to the edging on the truck bed. 'Someday,' he thought to himself. He stood on the passenger-side running board and noticed that the keys were still in the ignition. He looked around but didn't see anyone. Had the truck refused to start after being washed?

Richard recalled that on his first day on the job, a guy had pulled in, lifted the hood of a 1960 Chevy, and washed off the engine. When he got ready to leave, the car wouldn't start. The car wash owner had told the guy that he'd gotten water under his distributor cap. Richard wondered if new trucks still came equipped with distributor caps. He didn't think so. A few years ago, he'd taken a high school class in auto mechanics and didn't remember them.

Why would someone leave a new-model truck like this one with the keys in it? Maybe he should call the owner of the car wash or the Lakewood Police Department.

Less than ten minutes after Richard called, a Lakewood Police unit pulled into the car wash and waved him over. Richard stopped hosing down a wash bay and walked over to the police officer.

"That the truck you called about?" the officer asked.

"Yes, sir, it's been here since early morning. The keys are in it and no one has come back for it."

The uniformed officer walked over to the truck, wrote down the license number, and called the plate in to the police department.

"Nice truck," Vince Brown, the patrolman, said.

"You can say that again. I'd love to have a nice truck like this."

Vince studied Richard's behavior. It wouldn't be the first time in all his years that a kid took a cool vehicle out for a joy ride and then got spooked and ditched it. But not at the place where he worked, Vince reasoned. That didn't make sense. Nonetheless, he gathered Richard's information and asked the dispatcher to get any facts she could about the young man.

"Hmm, no one's reported it missing. You said the keys are in it?" the officer asked, rounding the back bumper and opening the driver-side door.

"Yep. I mean, yes sir. If I owned a truck as nice as this, I sure wouldn't leave it just sitting around with the keys in it," Richard said.

As he opened the driver-side door, Vince watched Richard, who was admiring the chrome on the front bumper. When Richard heard the door open, he looked up. "The seat is …." he said.

Before Richard could finish the sentence, Vince sat down and immediately jumped out.

"…soaked!" Richard said.

The officer turned around, trying to look at the seat of his pants. Richard saw the dark stain on the officer's uniform pants and suppressed a laugh.

"Can I get you a towel or … something, sir?" Richard asked.

"I'll call a tow truck," the officer said. "Yes, can you get me a towel so I don't get my car seat wet?"

The officer requested a tow truck to the address of the car wash. As he waited for the truck to arrive, he stood with his butt facing the sun, hoping that his uniform would dry.

"190, I have your 28 29 on the truck," the dispatcher radioed.

"Go ahead, PD, free to copy." Vince set his clipboard on the hood of his car and wrote down the information as the dispatcher gave it to him.

"The plate comes back to a 2019 Ford three-quarter-ton truck, black in color. The owner is Cody Lambert of Lakewood."

Detective Bob Barton had entered the police department just in time to hear Sandy's conversation about the truck and Cody's name.

"Just a minute, Sandy!" Bob said.

Sandy stopped and un-keyed the mic.

"Is Connor or Kate on duty?"

"No, they're both off. Do you need me to call them?" she asked.

"No, I'll head over to the car wash. Don't let the tow truck take that truck until Grant and I can look at it. Tell Vince to not let anyone touch the truck."

Detectives Bob Barton and Grant Harris rolled to a stop in front of the truck. They put on latex gloves. Officer Vince Brown walked over to the detectives.

"The kid said it's been here since this morning, when he got here," Vince said, hoping his uniform had dried by now.

Grant opened the truck door.

"Detective Harris, the seats are soaking wet," Vince said. "I wouldn't suggest sitting down."

"Wet?" Bob asked.

"The complete interior of the cab is wet," Vince said.

Bob looked over at Grant and nodded his head.

"Grant, give Connor and Kate a call. Make sure they bring Sundae with them. After that, have Sandy ask if the CIS team wants this towed to them or if they'll come out here," Bob said.

Overhearing Bob and the mention of the CIS team, Richard spun on his heels. He headed to the office and called the owner of the car wash.

Within fifteen minutes, Connor, Kate, and Sundae had arrived. Grant had already advised them on who owned the truck. Grant and Bob had opened both front doors, as well as the extended cab doors in the back. Connor and Kate got out of their vehicle. Through the open window, Connor held Lacey's jacket up to Sundae's face. Then he opened the car's back door and pointed to the truck's open doors. Kate and Connor pulled on their latex gloves.

"Pull down the tailgate, too," Connor called out to Bob, who did so.

Sundae jumped into the bed of the truck, sniffed around, and jumped out. Next, she searched the extended cab. From there, she jumped into the front seat. She wasn't showing any signs that she'd found anything. Connor was looking the truck over when Sundae jumped out of the vehicle.

"It's been hosed down, so she may not be able to pick up anything," Connor said to Kate, Bob, and Grant.

Sundae went underneath the truck and sniffed the undercarriage, starting at the rear and working her way forward. Once she got even with the passenger-side door, she sat and howled, signaling that she had found something. The four detectives looked under the truck but found nothing,

"Do you see anything?" Kate asked Connor. "Nothing, but she sure thinks that something's there. Let the CIS team give this a good going over and we'll see. Meanwhile, let's pay Cody Lambert a visit."

CHAPTER 15

Connor, with Sundae by his side, knocked loudly on Cody Lambert's front door. At the same time, Kate went to the back door and knocked. Bob and Grant each took a side of the house and went from window to window, peering inside. Sundae turned away from the door and faced the sidewalk.

"Can I help you?" called out a male voice from the front sidewalk.

Connor spun around. "Detective Connor Maxwell," he said, pulling out his ID and showing it to the man. "We're with the Lakewood Police Department. And you would be…"

"Neighbor. I live on the other side of the street. Name's Pete Dempsey. Lived here for twenty years," Pete said.

"Do you know the whereabouts of Mr. Lambert?" Connor asked.

"No, I haven't seen him …well, let's say for about a day or so."

"Pete, what's going on?" asked a petite, Irish-accented, red-haired woman in her seventies as she tapped Pete's shoulder.

"Why, they're looking for Cody," Pete answered as he turned and looked at the woman. "Detective, this is my wife, Maggie."

"This detective, is looking for Cody? He's such a sweet boy. I hope nothing's wrong with him," Maggie said, looking at Connor.

"I was just asking your husband if he knew where Cody is. When is the last time you saw him?" Connor asked.

"Oh, I haven't seen him in at least a day," Maggie responded.

"What about his truck? Have you seen it in the driveway?" Connor asked.

"No, haven't seen it or young Cody. You know, I think he blames himself."

Pete cut her response short. "Now, Mother, we shouldn't be telling things like this."

By this time, Bob, Grant, and Kate were also at the front of the house, listening to Connor's conversation the Dempseys.

"These are Detectives Stroup, Barton, and

Harris." Connor introduced them to the elderly couple.

Bob spoke up. "Pete, I was wondering … what are these purple bushes? I notice that almost every house has them. My wife, Bettie Jo, would love one in our backyard." Bob pointed toward the side of the house. He began walking toward that location. Pete followed him, leaving Maggie with the other detectives.

"Mrs. Dempsey, you said you thought Cody blames himself. What exactly did you mean by that?" asked Connor.

"Cody has been renting this house from us. He's a good boy. We have him over for Sunday dinner. He's like a son to us. Always pays his rent on time. He was quite smitten with that young girl who went missing."

Kate was busy writing down everything Mrs. Dempsey said into her notebook All the while, Bob kept Pete busy at the side of the house, asking about the care and soil conditions of the purple bushes.

"Why would he blame himself?" Connor asked.

"I really don't know, Detective Maxwell." Maggie seemed to be deep in thought.

"Has Cody ever left the area like this before?" Connor asked.

Mrs. Dempsey hesitated. "Why … no, not that I can ever remember. A fine young man."

Connor pulled out his business card and handed

it to Mrs. Dempsey. "When Cody comes back, would you give us a call, please?" he asked.

Connor, Kate, and Sundae entered G and R Welding Shop off of Main Street and asked to speak to the manager. Several minutes later, a man in his fifties came out of the office and extended a hand.

"I'm Jake Morrow, the owner and manager. How can I help you?"

Kate thought that Jake could have been Ed Asner's double.

"Mr. Morrow, I'm Detective Connor Maxwell and this is my partner, Detective Kate Stroup. We were given this as a place of employment for Cody Lambert. Can you tell us if he still works here?" Connor asked.

"Yes, he's one of my welders here," Jake responded.

"Is Cody here?"

"No, as a matter of fact, Cody never showed up for work Saturday or today," Jake said. "It's not like him to not call. If the kid's going to be ten minutes late, he calls."

"Any of his co-workers heard from him in the last few days?" Kate asked.

"Not that I know of. Have you checked with his sister?" Jake offered.

"Do you know if she lives in or around Lakewood?" Kate asked.

"She lives outside the city in the rural area."

"Would you by any chance have contact information for her?" Kate asked.

"As a matter of fact, if I remember correctly, she's his emergency contact. Let me go check."

A few minutes later, Jake returned with a slip of paper containing Cody's sister's name, phone number, and address. He handed it to Kate.

Connor and Kate thanked Jake, then headed over to the sister's house.

"Cody is moving up on my list of people of interest," Connor said.

"What doesn't make sense is that he doesn't look anything like the sketch Mrs. Kilgore gave us," Kate said.

"Do you think Cody wears size-twelve shoes?" Connor asked.

"I wasn't really paying attention to his shoe size," Kate said. "On the day Lacey was abducted, he was wearing what looked like steel-toed work boots. He was wearing the same thing when we asked him to come in for more questioning. The night you brought him in to the PD in his underwear, he had no shoes on."

"Wonder why he wouldn't report that fancy truck missing?" Connor asked.

Kate knew Connor wasn't asking a question so much as running things through his mind.

Connor and Kate drove past 68 Rural Route 2, the address Cody's boss had given them for his sister, Rebecca.

"Wow. Now, that's a nice place!" Connor said.

The horse ranch looked to be about twenty acres, with a white fence that stretched beyond the red stable. Horses grazed on the grassland. After turning around the unmarked unit, Connor pulled down a long driveway. Both sides had large brick columns with lights mounted on top. Trees and grass lined the driveway leading to the house. Connor almost missed the curve in the driveway as he admired the brick house, whose four large peaks jutted upward. The front of the house was meticulously landscaped.

"Either Rebecca is a drug lord or she married money," Connor said.

"She could have a great job, too," Kate pointed out as they got out of the unit. As they rang the bell, the three were dwarfed by the large oak door.

"My year's salary, and yours, probably couldn't even pay the property taxes on this place," Connor said.

A woman in her early thirties answered the door. She was well-dressed, with blonde, highlighted hair. "May I help you?"

Kate noticed that Connor seemed as taken with the woman as he was with the property.

"We're looking for Rebecca Kingston," Kate said.

"I'm Rebecca. What's this about?"

"I'm Detective Kate Stroup and this is my partner, Detective Connor Maxwell."

"And who are you?" The woman bent down and petted Sundae, who sat down, enjoying the attention.

"Sundae, like ice cream," Connor said as the woman fingered Sundae's badge.

"You must be a police dog." Rebecca stood and faced them. "What's this about?"

"We're looking for your brother, Cody. Do you have any idea where he is?" Connor asked.

Rebecca stepped back and opened the door to her home. "Why don't you all come in? May I get you something to drink and some water for Sundae?"

"Yes," Connor said as Kate quickly said, "No, thank you."

The three entered the finely decorated home. Rebecca motioned for them to sit, then sat down herself. She looked up and sighed heavily. "I picked him up the other night in Lakewood, drunk. He left work in the middle of the afternoon and went to a bar."

"So, does Cody have a drinking problem?" Connor asked.

"No, not at all. Well, he never has before. Our father was killed by a drunk driver."

"Rebecca," Kate started but was cut off.

"Please, just call me Becky."

"Becky, do you have any idea why or what led up to Cody drinking the other afternoon?" Connor asked.

"Well, as far as I could tell, Cody left work around three o'clock and went to this bar over on Main Street. I got a call from the owner, saying that Cody wasn't fit to drive. I drove over there and picked him up," Becky said.

"Did someone drive him to the bar or did he do it himself?" Kate asked.

"His truck wasn't at the bar when I got there. Maybe someone took him there, but I really have no idea."

"Rebecca … Becky … do you know where your brother is now?" Kate asked.

"I raised my brother after Dad was killed and Mom remarried. So, he looks up to me. He told me he needed some cash so he could get away for a while, to clear his head."

"Did you call him a cab or buy him a ticket?" Connor asked.

"He said he wanted to visit a friend out of state. I made him a pot of coffee and told him to go upstairs and shower. I laid some of my husband's clothes out for him to wear and some to take with him."

"Do you know this friend or where Cody went?" Kate asked.

"His name is Doug. I don't remember his last name. I called a cab to take him to the airport. I think the friend lives in Denver. Is Cody okay?" Becky was noticeably worried about her younger brother.

"We don't really know. His Ford pickup was found at a car wash, with the keys in the ignition, Saturday morning. Are you sure he went to the airport after he left here?" Connor asked.

"No, not a hundred percent. I called a cab, he left, and I assumed he got on a flight to visit his friend. I knew I shouldn't have let him go." Tears began streaming down Becky's face as she wrung her slender hands.

CHAPTER 16

Connor pulled the cover off Sundae's bed and tossed it into the washing machine. Sundae watched him put on a clean cover. She looked put out at having to wait while he placed her bed back in its usual place.

As he finished, his phone rang. "Maxwell," he answered.

"Connor, I'm sorry to bother you on your day off," the Lakewood dispatcher said. "Kate mentioned you were going hiking today, but a Ms. Kingston called and wanted to talk to you. I told her Kate was on duty but she wants to talk only to you."

"Oh, yes. Mrs. Kingston is Cody's sister. Did she leave a phone number?" Connor asked.

"No, she wants to talk with you at her house. She said you know where she lives."

"Okay, I'll take a drive over there. Maybe she heard from Cody."

Connor hung up the phone, pulled on his boots, and grabbed his car keys. Sundae looked up at him expectantly, knowing his usual routine on their day off.

"Do you want to go?" Connor crouched down to pet Sundae.

Sundae tilted her head from side to side, looking at him.

"Well, do you want to go or not? I know it's our day off, so if you want to stay home, your doggie door is open. You can lay out on the back porch and sunbathe."

With that, Sundae wagged her tail and scampered to the front door, her decision made.

Connor knocked on the front door of Becky's home, but to his surprise no one answered. Then he heard the sound of a horse's hooves on the driveway. Both he and Sundae turned to see Becky sitting atop a red dun quarter horse.

"Detective, I wasn't expecting you so soon. I was just starting my morning ride. Why don't you join me? I'll saddle up another horse for you. Come on." She motioned with her hand. "I saw those boots the other day and figured you must know how to ride a horse." Becky gave a flirtatious laugh and smiled. "Come on back to the stable and we can talk on the ride. I know Sundae will enjoy the walk alongside the horses."

"Okay, but just a short one. I haven't been on a horse since I lived on the ranch with my parents."

Becky had the stable hand saddle up one of her mares so that by the time they got to the stable, the horse was saddled and ready. Connor swung up into the saddle as Sundae looked up at him in confusion. Becky reined her horse toward a trail. Connor did the same and called out to Sundae to follow.

"So, Rebecca ... I mean, Becky ... what did you want to talk to me about?" Connor asked, hoping she had heard from Cody.

"I'm sure you want to know if Cody was back or if I'd heard from him," Becky said. She turned in the saddle and propped her forearm on the saddle horn, looking at Connor as the horses continued a slow, steady walk.

"I thought maybe that was why you called the police department."

"You cut right to the chase, don't you?" She laughed. "Just enjoy the ride, the clean air, and the view, Detective."

They rode to the top of a large, grassy knoll. Becky pivoted her horse, so Connor did the same.

From their vantage point, they were overlooking her horse ranch.

Becky swung her right leg over the horse and dismounted, then sat in the pasture. Connor did the same and Sundae ran to his side. The hill on which the three sat gave Connor a better look at the beautiful acreage stretching out before him.

"Beautiful place you and your husband own," Connor said, hoping to get her talking again

"Ex … ex-husband." Becky turned and looked at Connor.

"But you said the night you picked up Cody from the bar, you made him shower and then got some of your husband's clothes to wear. Plus, Cody's boss wrote "Mrs. Kingston" on the contact paper he gave us. I guess I'm confused," Connor said, playing with a blade of grass.

"Habit, I guess … the day you were here. And, when Cody took the job at the welding shop, I was a 'missus.' But Mr. Kingston wanted a younger Mrs. Kingston. Ten years younger, to be exact. She was looking for money; he was looking to get laid."

"Sounds like the Bermuda Triangle." Connor smiled and leaned back on his elbows, relaxing.

"And you. Is there a Mrs. Maxwell at home waiting for you?"

"No, divorced. I casually date once in a while," Connor said.

"What about Kate? She seemed very protective the day you all were here."

"Hmm … Kate. At first, it was a policy of the department that people in the same department couldn't date, marry, or live together."

"And?" Becky asked.

"Well, they loosened up that policy. We go out now and then but we both love our jobs. And I think she feels uncomfortable getting into a serious relationship, as we're partners at the police department. I heard she went out with a guy from the Natick Sheriff's Department last week. I also heard that she had a good time. Anyway, that's according to the rumor mill at the department."

Becky watched him closely. A lock of his dark brown hair danced across his forehead.

"So, back to your brother. Has Cody come back or called?" Connor turned on his side to pet Sundae's neck.

Becky remained silent for a few minutes, then picked up a small twig and broke it in two. Connor watched her body language. The softness of her facial expression hardened slightly.

"He did call me last night. I told him his truck was found in a carwash, with the keys in it."

"What did he say to that?"

"He told me he drove it to the bar. When the bartender told him he was in no shape to drive, he had the guy call me."

"Did the bartender take his keys?"

"I asked him that and he said he couldn't remember. He said he was upset when he got there, so he may have left them in his truck."

"I can go by the bar and find out later," Connor said.

"Detective, Cody feels you're focusing your investigation around him and not looking for the person who took that woman." Becky's blue eyes starred into Connor's eyes, seeking the truth.

"Becky, I have to admit, Cody has been at several places that lead us to believe he's a person of interest. I can assure you and Cody that we check every tip that comes in."

"So, is my brother on your list of subjects or just a 'person of interest,' as you officers have said many times?" Becky's tone demanded an answer.

Suddenly, Connor felt uncomfortable. He could see that Becky was more of a mother figure to Cody than a sister.

"Becky, do you mind answering one question for me?"

"That depends on the question."

"Do you know Cody's shoe size? You did mention that he lived with you after your mother remarried."

Becky thought for a minute before responding. "I'm not sure what his shoe size is. What does that have to do with whoever took that poor woman?"

"Just curious," Connor answered.

"Detective, he wears a size twelve. Any further questions about Cody, his truck, and his whereabouts will need to be addressed to our attorney, Mr. Martin A. Kingston. Yes, in case you're wondering, he's my ex-husband."

CHAPTER 17

Connor slammed his palms on the steering wheel in frustration. "Why didn't I recognize the name 'Kingston'?" he muttered in frustration.

Martin Kingston—*the* Martin Kingston—had one of the largest defense law firms, not only in Lakewood but also in the entire state. Kingston Law Firm commercials aired several times every night on the six and ten o'clock news. The commercials featured none other than Martin himself, dressed in a Brioni Vanquish II suit. Connor had heard that those suits cost forty-three thousand dollars, but he thought the figure must have been exaggerated. One night, he came home from the courthouse and Googled it. Sure enough, that was the price. Word had it that Martin also wore a Louis Vuitton crocodile belt that cost over three thousand. Once you added the Ralph

Lauren cashmere silk tie to the mix, Connor figured that Martin's daily attire cost more than his own Toyota Tacoma truck parked in the garage.

Connor remembered thinking that the name had sounded familiar when Cody's boss had given it to him and Kate on that slip of paper. However, Connor had been so focused on the truck abandoned at the car wash and the fact that Cody hadn't shown up at home or work that he hadn't given the name a second thought. As for the sprawling ranch and the amazing house, now it all made sense. Kingston must have given Rebecca—or Becky, as she preferred—the ranch, the ponies, and a boatload of cash while he went out and corralled a much younger filly to put in his new stable.

Connor could understand Becky wanting to protect her brother. It was simply human nature. What he didn't understand was why Cody felt the need to run off to Denver—if that was where he really was. Was Cody running scared because he was guilty...or was he simply running scared? Nonetheless, Connor had learned that Cody wore a size twelve shoe, which put another checkmark beside Cody's name.

Connor hung his sport coat on the back of his chair and took a seat at his desk. "Good morning to you, too," he said as he looked over at Kate.

"What the hell were you thinking?" she asked, an annoyed look on her face.

"What are you talking about?"

"The DA received a call this morning from Martin Kingston. You know, *the* Martin Kingston?" Kate said. "The sergeant called me into the office and wanted to know why we were harassing Kingston's ex-wife. Something about you going out to *his* ranch and going riding with *his* ex-wife and trying to get information about Cody."

"Are you finished?" Connor said calmly.

Kate was silent.

"The PD received a call on my day off. Rebecca Kingston wanted to talk to me, and only me." Connor paused. "I drove out to the ranch. When I got there, I knocked several times but there was no answer. I was about to leave when she rode up on a horse. Said she needed to talk to me but was leaving on her morning ride. If I wanted to hear what she had to say, I had to go with her," Connor said.

"Did you find Cody at her house? Did he come back?"

"No, but once we got on the subject of Cody, she answered my questions. He wasn't back in Lakewood and he did call her the night before. She told him about his truck so that he could file a claim with his insurance company."

"Anything else?" Kate snapped.

"He wears a size twelve shoe." Connor looked over at Kate. "Are you upset about the sergeant and Martin Kingston, or are you upset that I went for a ride with Becky?" he asked.

"Don't flatter yourself, Detective Maxwell!" Kate pushed her chair away from the desk. Sundae got up and ran toward Kate, thinking they were all leaving. When Connor didn't get up, Sundae returned to his side as he watched Kate storm out of the office.

Kate walked through the dispatch room.

"What was all that about?" asked Sandy Curtis, looking up from her computer and microphone at the dispatch desk. "I heard the yelling all the way down here."

Kate looked around and shook her head. "Men!"

Sandy didn't reply as Kate hit the buzzer unlocking the metal security door and exited the police department. Kate walked out to the parking lot, unlocked her unmarked car, and sat there thinking. Was she mad that Connor had gone out to see Rebecca by himself, or that they'd gone for a horseback ride? Rebecca Kingston was beautiful; she was wealthy and had a figure to die for. Kate had noticed Becky's interest in Connor when they'd talked to her the other day. She'd have had to be blind not to notice.

But did she have the right to be upset? After all, she'd gone on a date with a guy from the Natick Sheriff's Department. Connor didn't know anything about it ... or did he? Kate knew that personal things get around, even if you don't want them to. Had Connor and Becky simply gone for a horseback ride, or had there been more to that afternoon?

As Kate sat there, she realized she was wrong. She and Connor had gone on a few dates. Kate had spent a night or two at his house and he at hers. They went to dinner, where most of the time they talked shop, discussing one case or another. They had talked about it and decided to keep things casual. As partners, they were worried that a relationship would get in the way of their work.

Also, Kate knew that Connor had trouble letting go of work. In a past case, he had never been able to find the victim to help create closure for the father. Kate knew that Connor blamed himself for not being able to find the woman. Connor was like that; he let things weave themselves deep inside himself, to the point that he couldn't let go. Nevertheless, deep within her heart, Kate knew she was in love with the man. The date with the deputy sheriff the other night had simply been something to do. The fact was, she'd thought of Connor the entire time, wishing she were with him instead. Nonetheless, she had a job to do and so did Connor.

CHAPTER 18

The Lakewood Police Department believed they had a credible tip from two hikers who had seen, in the nearby mountains, someone they believed fit the description of the toothless man. The police set up a base camp at the edge of the mountains. The state police and the county sheriff's department joined the Lakewood Police to combine their efforts in the search. Given the amount of terrain to cover in the mountains blanketed with Gambel and Emory oaks, pinyon and ponderosa pines, and alligator juniper trees, visibility was limited, to say the least.

The Lakewood Police brought out several folding tables and spread maps of the mountains across them. Connor placed fist-sized rocks on the corners of each map, as a light autumn breeze had begun to blow. He had divided the area into three quadrants, one for each department to search. Each two-person team had to sign in and out when they left and returned. Each team member carried a hand-held radio to keep in contact with the others. Connor left with only Sundae by his side. After Kate's fiery outburst back at the office, he thought it best. Kate teamed up with Bob Barton and Grant Harris.

At lunchtime, volunteers brought sandwiches, hot coffee, cold drinks, and bags of chips. Kate looked around the makeshift camp but didn't see Connor or Sundae. Casually, she walked over to the table with the clipboard that held the sign-in sheets. She glanced down at the log and saw that Connor hadn't returned for lunch.

"Something you're looking for, Detective Stroup?" the sergeant asked.

"No, nothing."

"He's still out in the field. Hasn't come in for lunch. You two having issues?" asked the sergeant.

"No, not at all," Kate said and walked away.

Around one o'clock the teams began heading back up the mountain trails. Before Kate left, she turned to the sergeant.

"You know, the department really needs a drone. We could cover so much more territory that way," she said.

"I asked for one in this year's budget but it was declined."

"Does the sheriff's department have one, or the state police?

"I think the state police have one. You might ask Theo Atwell. He's over there," the sergeant said, pointing to an officer wearing a black uniform with gray epaulets and a gray stripe running down the outside of his pant leg.

Kate walked over to Theo, who was about five-nine she guessed—about the same height as Connor. 'Damn it!' she thought to herself. 'Why do I always compare other men to Connor?' Nonetheless, Theo was quite handsome—easy on a lady's eyes. Dark brown hair, broad shoulders, and a warm, inviting smile. Come to think of it, he could have passed for Connor's brother. The last name wasn't the same, so Kate discounted that idea.

"I was wondering, by any chance, if your department has a drone we could use." Kate asked.

Theo smiled at her and extended his right hand. "Theo Atwell. And you are...?"

"I'm sorry. Detective Kate Stroup." Kate blushed and shook his hand.

"Pleased to meet you, Detective Stroup."

"Kate. Please call me Kate." She pulled out one of her business cards and handed it to him.

"With the Lakewood Police Department," Theo said with a smile.

Kate's cheek's flushed with embarrassment.

"Detective, I'll see if our drone pilot can assist," Theo said. "If he can, I'll let the base camp know."

"Thank you."

Kate walked away, thinking, 'That was embarrassing as hell.'

She was back on the trail with Barton and Harris when the radio silence broke.

"Be advised, in further talking to the two hikers, we have ascertained that the man they saw does not fit the description of the unknown man with missing front teeth or Cody Lambert. At this time, one of our officers is interviewing the man whom the hikers reported."

Connor heard the radio transmission and turned around. His stomach growled, as he'd missed lunch. Sundae still had her nose to the ground and her tail up, sniffing along the trail. She stopped and pawed at a pile of leaves beyond the trail, near a line of pine trees.

Connor walked over to her. "Let's go get some lunch, Sundae." He looked down at the pile of leaves and pine needles, then brushed away some of the debris with the tip of his boot. Sundae stuck her nose farther into the pile of leaves. Connor bent down and began digging through the pile of leaves with both hands. Then he felt something.

"What the hell…" His sentence trailed off as he carefully lifted a human hand.

There, in the quietness of a lonely forest, lay a body, which had been discarded like yesterday's trash. No one to place flowers upon the grave. Only trees surrounded the grave, like sentinels watching over it.

Quickly, he grabbed his radio off his belt.

"Fifteen to base." Connor waited for the reply.

"Fifteen, go ahead,"

"Sarge, I have a body buried under some leaves and brush."

From his smartphone, Connor gave the coordinates of his location. It would take the remaining officers at the base camp about forty-five minutes to get to his location. While he waited, Connor carefully removed the leaves from the shallow grave. Without disturbing the soil, he found another hand attached to a wrist.

As the group of officers approached his location, Bob Barton said, "The sergeant already called the coroner. Is it Lacey?"

"The body is pretty decomposed. I guess we'll have to wait to compare dental records, if the skull is under there. Did you call out the CIS team, too?" Connor asked.

"Done. Not to worry."

"I had Sundae check this area in case it's a dumping ground for other bodies, but nothing so far," Connor said. He glanced around the wooded area as several Lakewood Police officers stretched crime scene tape around trees, roping off the area. "Thanks," Connor said to the officers as they finished.

Connor and Kate waited in silence until the CIS team showed up.

"We need anything you can dig up," Connor told Eric Martinez of the CIS team.

"You know we will," Eric said as Connor turned to leave. "Oh, by the way, it's a media circus down there," Eric added as he set down a large container with his tools.

"They're like flies at a barbecue," Connor said.

Connor, Kate, and Sundae walked down the trail together.

"Listen, I'm sorry … about this morning." Kate waited for a response but none came. "I was out of line."

Connor kept walking, then stopped and looked in her direction. "No. I shouldn't have gone riding with Becky."

"My grandfather used to say, 'You can take the boy out of the country but you can never take the country out of the boy,'" Kate said.

Connor laughed. "It was nice to go horseback riding. I enjoyed that part of it for sure."

"Is there an us?" Kate asked.

Connor pushed back the branch of a large tree.

As Connor, Kate, and Sundae came through the opening in the trees to the base camp, Candy Martin, a local TV reporter, thrust a microphone in their faces.

"Detective Maxwell, can you confirm that the body that was found up there is that of Lacey Warner?"

"No comment," Connor said, pushing the microphone out of his way.

"Detective Stroup, what about you? Can you confirm that the body is that of Lacey Warner?"

"Like Detective Maxwell just said, there is no comment at this time."

CHAPTER 19

Connor pulled his unmarked car into the parking lot at the Lakewood Police Department, followed by Kate. Zachary Bryn stood outside the entrance to the police department. He looked between Connor and Kate, trying to read their expressions.

"Was it her ... was it Lacey? I heard a report on the radio that you found a body up in the mountains." Zachary's voice cracked with emotion.

Kate took Zachary by the arm and walked him toward a metal bench away from the doorway. Connor and Sundae followed.

"It was her, wasn't it?" Zachary's eyes flooded with tears that spilled down his cheeks. Kate sat on the bench and Zachary sat next to her.

Connor spoke. "Zach, at this point all I can tell

you is that what Sundae and I found this afternoon was human remains. Our CSI team has the proper tools to remove the remains so as not to disturb any evidence left behind." Connor paused and bent down to look Zachary in the eyes. "Honestly, at this point, I couldn't tell you if it was a male or a female. I only found the hands, which were uncovered up to the wrists. They were left in a shallow grave covered by leaves and pine needles. I know it's hard, but I need you to just wait along with us. The coroner will look over the body and compare dental records as well as anything else left in or around the gravesite to help us piece together who this is and how long they've been out there."

Zachary was visibly shaking as he looked at his boots. Sundae moved over toward Zach. When he saw the beagle, he began to pet her, which seemed to help relieve some of the stress he was feeling.

"Zach, as soon as we find out anything, we'll tell you. You have my word on it." Kate put her arm around Zachary's shoulder.

The big man turned his head to Kate as she pulled him closer. Sundae jumped up on the bench on the opposite side of Zach and placed her body against his.

"Why? Why did this have to happen to her … to her kids?" Zachary's cries were muffled into Kate's shoulder.

"I wish I knew," Kate said as she held Lacey's brother.

It was times like this that Connor wished he'd chosen another profession. If they could deliver good news all the time, that would be so much better. All too often, detectives were the bearers of bad news—or no news at all.

After work, Connor took Sundae home and fed her dinner. Once she had finished, Sundae left the kitchen without giving Connor a second look. Connor thought to himself that it was the same look his ex-wife had given him when she'd said, "I don't want to talk about it. I just need to be left alone." Connor watched Sundae as she walked through the doggie door to the screened-in porch and curled up on her favorite chair. He wondered how much a thirteen-inch beagle could understand. Based on the way she'd moved in toward Zachary earlier that day, she must have been able to sense something. Connor walked out to the porch and sat in the chair next to Sundae. He picked up a stuffed teddy bear. "Do you want to go play?" Connor stood up, holding the bear.

Sundae looked up, then placed her head back down.

"Okay, I understand." Connor set Jack the bear beside her on the chair.

Connor remembered that, in the police academy, officers were trained to detach themselves from crimes. The training officer told them that they would go crazy if they didn't. Yet how could Connor teach Sundae to detach from all the hardship they encountered? Was all this upsetting her, or was she able to just zone out on her porch, as he had seen her do so many times like this?

Connor was supposed to meet Kate, Bob, and Grant at the grill. Instead, he texted Kate to tell her that Sundae wasn't herself and that he'd be staying home with her. He then went back out to the porch, picked up Sundae, and sat with her on a cushioned glider. He didn't talk—just held her and pet her until they both fell asleep.

Connor's cell phone woke him up from a deep sleep. It was Alistair Gordon. His daughter, Mia, had disappeared several years earlier, while Connor and Kate were investigating a series of murders. Mia's body had never been recovered and Connor continued looking for her every chance he could.

"Detective Maxwell, it sounds like I woke you up. I'm so sorry, but I heard on the news that a body was found up in the mountains. Was it…?" Dr. Gordon's voice cracked and he broke down before he could finish his sentence.

"Dr. Gordon, I don't know yet. Our CIS team is working it along with Malcolm Greenblatt, the coroner. It'll take them some time to determine the identity of the remains. I found only the hands and wrists, which are so badly decomposed that I was unable to tell if they were male or female. Policy states we have to call in the professionals to remove the remains and put together the puzzle pieces. Dr. Gordon, I'm sorry that I have nothing yet to tell you. I wish I did," Connor said.

"You'll call me if..."

"Dr. Gordon, you know I will. One way or the other."

Connor, Kate, and Sundae stood beside a stainless-steel table in the coroner's office.

"I called you over here today to show you what I've determined."

Malcolm Greenblatt, M.E., was the county coroner. He was a rotund man with a gruff voice. Covering his wrinkled street clothes was a white lab coat with his name neatly embroidered over the pocket.

Connor watched as Malcolm slowly removed the white sheet from the remains. Kate gasped and Connor swallowed hard. Connor's eyes locked on the short strand of barbed wire with a wooden dowel attached to each end. This was known as a Mexican bow tie and it had been used to strangle the victim. Kate and Connor had investigated a serial killer who had used this technique on his victims several years earlier.

"This isn't Lacey. I compared dental records already," Malcolm said.

"Is it Mia…?"

Before Connor could finish, Malcolm spoke. "I knew you'd ask that." The doctor looked down at the remains and shook his head. "No, this isn't Mia Gordon. I also checked her dental records. At this point, we have no idea who this person is. I will submit my data to the database to see if we can find a match. Maybe we'll find something, maybe not. Only time will tell. I can tell you, with hips as narrow as these, this is probably a male." Dr. Greenblatt pointed to the pelvic area. "One thing is certain. He left his calling card with the barbed wire around the neck."

"While we don't know who this is, we do know who did it," Connor said.

"We always figured there were more victims out there. We just had no idea how many," Kate added.

"Even from the grave, that bastard is still haunting me with his killing spree," Connor said.

Kate looked over at Connor. "Why don't you call Mia's dad and I'll call Zach?" she said. "We can tell them that these aren't the remains of their loved ones. We also need to let the press know. They're calling the PD every day."

"I'll call Bob and Grant. I'm sure they'll talk to the press for us," Connor said.

Connor drove over to Dr. Gordon's house to

deliver the news that the remains were not those of his daughter, Mia. As he drove, dispatch called to tell him that Cody Lambert had returned to Lakewood. Cody and his attorney wanted to set up a time to talk to Connor and Kate.

Connor looked over at Sundae and said, "It's about time!"

CHAPTER 20

Connor pulled into Dr. Gordon's driveway. His memories of this place pulled him back like a disobedient child being pulled along by his mother. Connor and Kate had worked a case involving serial killer Jared Hobbs. Dr. Gordon's daughter, Mia, had been abducted by Hobbs and never found. It may have been his imagination, but Connor felt an emptiness engulf the Gordon home now.

Before Connor was out of the car, Dr. Gordon had come out and walked halfway down the driveway. He slowed as if his legs were weighted down more with each step. When Dr. Gordon got close to Connor, he stopped. It was as if the worst of his fears would come true if he got too close. The two men stood facing each other like gunslingers in an old-time western. Neither took a step forward.

"Was it her? Did you find Mia?" Dr. Gordon finally spoke, his voice cracking with emotion before he broke down.

"Dr. Gordon, the body I found was not Mia," Connor said. He walked over and put his arms around the other man. "I promised to let you know, no matter what."

"You're sure, it's not … her?" The doctor's voice pleaded and his eyes begged for answers.

"Dr. Gordon, we're sure. Dental records confirmed it."

Without another word, Dr. Gordon turned around. His shoulders slumped as though they were weighted down with a burden too heavy to carry. Slowly, he walked back into his house. Connor stood and watched the front door close behind the doctor.

In the interview room, Cody Lambert sat next to his attorney and ex-brother-in-law, Martin Kingston, as Kate and Connor looked through the one-way glass.

"I wonder why he didn't ask for Kingston the night of Mrs. Kilgore's home invasion," Kate said.

Connor didn't respond but he'd been thinking the same thing.

The two walked into the room and took seats across from Cody and Kingston.

"Thank you for coming in. We'll be recording

this interview today." Connor reached over and started the audio recording device. The video was already rolling. "Today, present are Cody Lambert, his attorney Martin Kingston, Detective Kate Stroup, and myself, Detective Connor Maxwell. Cody, can you tell us when you last saw your 2019 Ford truck?"

Cody looked over at Kingston, who nodded for Cody to answer the question.

"Last Thursday. I drove to that little bar, the one next to the post office on Main Street, and had a few drinks."

"Do you usually go there to drink?" Connor asked.

"No, I usually never drink or go to bars," Cody answered.

"The bartender told us you had six beers," Connor said.

"I guess I was upset."

"What was upsetting you?"

"Her," Cody blurted out.

"Her who?" Connor asked.

"Lacey. I'm getting blamed for ... whatever and I loved her," Cody said.

"Cody, I think this interview is over." Martin Kingston stood and straightened his expensive dress slacks and tie.

"No! They need to know ... I loved her. I looked forward to seeing her every morning. Hell, I finally worked up the courage to ask her out that day. But she wasn't there when I arrived," Cody said.

"Cody, was Lacey ever in your truck?" Connor asked.

"Detectives, as I said, this interview is over. Cody, let's go," Martin Kingston said impatiently, his piercing eyes as cold as an icicle in January.

"No, she was never in my truck," Cody said as Kingston pulled Cody's chair from the table, forcing Cody to go with him.

"Unless my client is under arrest, we're leaving."

Cody followed Martin Kingston to the door, then spun around to face the detectives. "I didn't do it! While you're focusing on me, the real killer is out there," Cody said as Kingston opened the door and forcefully pushed him out, then slammed the door behind them.

After they left, Sandy knocked on the door and opened it. "Thought I might find you two in here. The coroner called. He identified the body that you found," Sandy said.

"And?" Connor asked

"Jared Allen Hobbs, Jr.," Sandy said, looking up from the notepad where she had written the name.

"That bastard murdered his own son?" Connor's voice was incredulous.

"When we worked that case, Jared and his wife had no children," Kate said.

"He had been married before. Remember, it ended in divorce?"

"I need to take Carlos and Pebbles to their tracking class. I'll be back here by four, but if you need me before then, I can have one of the patrolmen pick up Carlos."

After dropping off Carlos and Pebbles at their tracking class, Connor and Sundae went straight to the basement of the Lakewood Police Department and requested all the records from the Jared Hobbs case. Connor grabbed one of the metal trolleys that the records department used to deliver requested files to officers upstairs. He loaded up the files, signed the clipboard to indicate that he was taking them, and headed to his desk upstairs. Some of the paper was already starting to yellow from age and it smelled musty. The pages had colored flags and side notes.

Connor saw a page with Kate's handwriting on it. He remembered that she had asked him the question, "What about us?" right before that pushy reporter, Candy Martin, had shoved her microphone into their faces. He made a mental note to ask Kate if they could talk later.

Back at his desk, Connor sifted through the files until he found the banking records. Jared's wife, through her attorney, had turned them over to the police department after Jared had been caught and jailed. As he started re-examining statements,

Connor wondered whether they could have missed something. Suddenly, a figure stood out: a one-time payment to Jared himself for a hundred and fifty thousand dollars. It was from an insurance company. Could it have been the motive for Jared to kill his own son?

Connor found the phone number for Jared's previous wife and dialed it.

"I'm looking for Mrs. Hobbs."

"This is Mrs. Hobbs. But, if you're trying to sell me anything, forget it!" the woman said in an unfriendly voice.

"Are you Alice Hobbs who was married to Jared Hobbs?"

"That bastard was arrested. I heard he died in prison."

"Mrs. Hobbs, my name is Connor Maxwell. I'm a detective with the Lakewood Police Department. Did you and Jared have a son by the name of Jared, Jr.?"

"Yes and no. Why do you ask?"

"Mrs. Hobbs, which is it? Yes or no?" Connor persisted.

"Jared had a son from an old relationship. Jared Jr. lived with us. Until..." she trailed off, as if in thought. "Jared left shortly after we divorced. I lost track of the kid. Assumed he was living with his father and his new wife."

"Thank you for the information."

"If the kid's in trouble, I want nothing to do with this, you understand."

Connor hung up and flipped through the contacts in the old file on Jared Hobbs. His finger came to rest on Kristen Hobbs' phone number.

"Hello."

"Kristen, this is Detective Connor Maxwell. I hope you remember me."

"I don't think I'll ever forget."

Connor knew Kristen had been completely shocked by her husband's secret life.

"When we first interviewed you, you said that you and Jared never had kids. Did you know about a child he had named Jared, Jr.?"

"Oh, yes. He lived with us for about three months, but Jared told me that he wanted to move back to Alice's. She was Jared's first wife. He said Jared, Jr. liked the schools better there in Springfield. Jared also told me that Alice wasn't his biological mother, but I can't remember if he ever gave me his real mother's name."

"Kristen, thank you again for the information." Connor hung up before she could ask why he wanted to know.

He checked the clock. It was six-thirty—just enough time to return the files to the basement and pick up Carlos and Pebbles from class. After loading everything back on the trolley, he sent a brief text to Kate and copied Bob and Grant:

"Talked to Alice Hobbs and Kristen Hobbs. Each thought Jared's son, Jared, Jr., was with the other and didn't think anything of it. Neither was Jared, Jr.'s mother. Talk to you more about it in the morning. Kate, left note on your desk. Leaving now to pick up Carlos and Pebbles from class."

Connor got a quick reply from Bob and Grant, noting that even from the grave, Jared was haunting them.

Next, Connor sent a private text to Kate, asking her to meet for dinner. She hadn't answered by the time Connor pulled into the training camp. Everyone had left except the instructor, Carlos, and Pebbles. Connor opened the door and Sundae bounded out to greet Pebbles and Carlos. The two beagles ran around the training area, chasing each other.

Connor laughed. "She had a tough week. She really needed this," he said to the instructor.

Once back in the unmarked car, Connor pulled out his phone. Still no message from Kate.

CHAPTER 21

When Connor hadn't heard from Kate, he called her cell phone. His call went straight to voicemail. 'It's not like Kate to not answer her phone,' he thought. A sense of worry began to creep into his mind. Without a second thought, he picked up his phone and dialed the police department's non-emergency line.

"Lakewood Police Department, how may I assist?" the dispatcher asked in a pleasant voice.

"Jess, this is Connor. Have you heard from Detective Stroup?"

Jessie clicked away on her keyboard, then came back on the line.

"Yes, she was at Zachary Bryn's house. Then she called in that she was heading back to the PD. I received a call for her from Officer Theo Atwell at the state police. He asked for Kate to call him. I gave her his phone number. Shortly after that, she called in that she was finished for the night."

"Atwell … Atwell," Connor repeated out loud, trying to place the name. "She did call and log out for the night?"

"Yes, sir, she did. Did you want me to get a message to Detective Stroup?"

"No, I'll talk to her in the morning. Thanks, Jess. Call me if you need me."

As the long shadows of evening gave way to darkness, Connor stood and turned on a tableside lamp, still wracking his brain as to who Theo Atwell was and what he wanted with Kate. He fed Sundae and then decided to head out for dinner anyway. He reasoned that if Kate wanted to join him for dinner, she would have called or texted. Something must have come up. Connor called Carlos and asked the young boy if he and his grandmother would like to join him for dinner.

Connor opened the door to Angelo's Pizzeria and followed Carlos into the restaurant.

"Too bad your grandmother didn't feel up to coming," Connor said as the hostess stepped forward with two menus in hand.

"I don't think she likes pizza," Carlos said.

"What's this I hear about your grandmother not

liking pizza?" the hostess said, joking with Carlos, who blushed as she ushered them to a table.

Connor noticed a man in a state police uniform, sitting at a corner table tucked away from the other tables. He then realized that Kate was sitting across from the officer. They were laughing and seemed to be having a good time.

"Is this table okay?" the hostess asked with a smile. "Sir?" She looked at Connor when he didn't sit down.

Carlos pulled on Connor's sleeve to get his attention.

"Actually." Connor looked around and spotted a table on the opposite side of the room. "Maybe that would be better." Connor pointed to an empty table.

He wished he could just leave. If Carlos hadn't been with him, he would have. However, Connor knew how much Carlos loved pizza.

After the hostess seated them, Connor found himself glancing over at Kate. Was this Theo, the state police officer who had called for her this afternoon? Were they on a date?

Halfway through their dinner, Carlos was telling Connor, between bites of pizza, how great Pebbles was doing in the tracking class. Connor looked up and saw Kate coming toward them. He quickly averted his gaze, but it was too late. She was on her way to the ladies' room, which was behind Connor and Carlos's table, when she spotted Connor.

"Popular place," Kate said.

"Hi, Detective Stroup. Are you joining us, now?" Carlos asked with excitement.

"Ah, no. I was just getting ready to leave," Kate said. She was answering Carlos but looking at Connor.

One word was running through Connor's mind over and over again, like a mudslide running down a steep hill with nothing to contain it. That word was "awkward!"

"Have you two been here long?" Kate asked

Nothing Connor could think to say would come out correctly.

Carlos spoke up. "We were going to sit over there," he turned in his seat and pointed to the first table. "But Connor saw you talking to that state policeman and asked to be seated over here."

Connor thought that Carlos hadn't seen Kate and figured he could maneuver himself and Carlos out of the restaurant without being seen. Connor had to hand it to him—the kid had an eye for things.

Kate looked at Connor, who would have slid under the table if he could have. Frankly, she felt the same way. She excused herself and went to the ladies' room. Connor quickly requested a box for the leftover pizza and walked up to the register to pay. Just as he pulled his card from his wallet, Theo Atwell met Kate at the door and they walked out together. Kate followed Theo to his patrol unit.

Connor and Carlos exited quickly and then got into Connor's truck.

"Is that Ms. Kate's new boyfriend?" Carlos asked, turning and looking at the couple standing by the black state police car.

"I don't know, buddy. I don't know."

The Lakewood Airport was not very busy at ten-thirty at night. Colin stepped out of arrival gate number five and slowly strolled toward ground transportation. When he came alongside a glass picture frame and caught his own reflection, he smiled. Now he had teeth. Although they were implants, he thought his smile looked fantastic. Plus, while he was in Denver, he'd purchased a lot of new clothes—all bought and paid for with his daddy's credit card, along with the hotel stay. He looked like a new man. But were the clothes, the new hairstyle, and the teeth enough to leave his past demons behind him?

Colin was still very much addicted to porn. He had tried to stop watching it. If only a woman would be interested in him, then he could have a real life, not the fantasy one he watched on TV. He did manage to talk to one lady in Denver. She even acted like she was interested in him, until they were outside in the parking lot. When he tried to press her against her car, she pulled away from him, though not before slapping him squarely in the face. Colin shook that thought from his mind, then walked outside and grabbed a cab.

As they passed the bar on Main Street, he saw the flashing neon sign. He told the driver to turn around and leave him at the bar.

The old dive was crowded but Colin found a seat at the bar. He stowed his duffle bag on the floor at his feet and ordered a beer. After his seventh beer and a whiskey chaser, the bartender asked if Colin was driving.

"Nope, don't own a car!" Colin said in a drunken slur. "But I'll have another whiskey and one for my buddy here." Colin pointed to a short, dark-haired man in his forties, who had just sat down to his right.

Colin downed the whiskey in one gulp. Then a show about unsolved crimes came on the old TV over the bar. Lacey's image flashed across the screen. Colin squinted while looking at the TV.

"I know her!" Colin belched as he watched the television as if in a world of his own.

The man for whom Colin had purchased the drink clearly did not have the same amount of booze in his system as Colin did. He listened to the drunk sitting next to him.

"What a bitch she was. Had to tie her to my bed to…" His words seemed to slip off into the night air.

"Need to take a piss." The short man sitting next to Colin slid off his stool and quickly went down the narrow hallway toward the restrooms.

He fished his cell phone out of his pocket and dialed 911.

"911. What's your emergency?" the Lakewood dispatcher asked.

"Ah, I'm at the bar next to the Lakewood Post Office. There's … ah … there's a guy. He's really drunk. And, well, a show came on TV about a murder here in Lakewood. He said he had the lady tied to his bed."

"What's your name?"

"My name is Ned. Look, I don't know him."

"Ned, what is your last name?"

"Ned Ortiz, but I don't know who this guy is!"

"Ned, I'll have officers there in minutes. Stall him if he tries to leave. Do whatever you can. I'll call the bar and see if they can help. Just stay put."

Jess ended the call and dispatched two uniformed officers to the bar. She looked up and dialed the bar's phone number.

CHAPTER 22

Jess listened as the phone rang with no answer at Moe's Bar. "No, this can't be happening. Answer the phone!" she said to herself.

Looking at the digital clock on her computer, she knew it was late but quickly made the decision to call Connor's home phone number. Jess prided herself on her ability to multitask. As she waited for Connor to pick up, she keyed her microphone.

"98, be advised that I have no answer at Moe's Bar."

"10-4 PD."

Connor picked up on the third ring. "Hello."

"Connor, this is Jess. I think someone spotted Lacey's killer."

"Where, when?"

"Moe's Bar. I have two uniforms en route as we

speak. I told the guy who called to try to keep him there if he could. I called the bar but no one is answering."

"On my way," Connor said as his bare feet hit the floor and he disconnected the call.

Colin passed Ned, the man who'd been sitting beside him, in the hallway on his way to use the restroom. Ned turned and watched him enter the men's room. Then Ned returned to his seat and noticed a duffle bag wedged between the bar and the stool where the man had been sitting. Quickly, Ned leaned down and saw a stamped airline boarding pass sticking out of a side pocket. The name on the pass was Colin Bolton, seat 12A. Ned grabbed his pen and wrote the name on a bar napkin, which he quickly put in his pocket.

The bartender came back. "Refill, buddy?"

"No, hey ... we need to stall the guy next to me as long as we can," Ned said.

The bartender looked to Ned's left, then his right. Both stools were empty.

"Right," the bartender said sarcastically. "Sure. Will do, will do, Captain."

Colin came out of the men's room and fished through his pockets for some change. He put the money into the old payphone on the wall and called a cab. He said he'd be waiting outside.

Colin walked back to his barstool as Ned leaned over the bar, attempting to get the bartender's attention. Then Colin picked up his duffle bag and walked outside.

The cool night air was just what he needed to clear his head. Several minutes later, the cab pulled into the parking lot. The driver had to wait before pulling back out onto Main Street. As he did, two Lakewood police cars pulled into the parking lot. Colin turned and watched them.

Inside, Ned was frantic when he realized the duffle bag was gone. He ran down the hallway toward the restrooms and bumped into a young couple who were kissing in the hallway.

"Hey, watch it, buddy!" the young man said to Ned.

Ned burst through the men's room door and looked under all the stalls with doors. Colin was gone—or, at least, he wasn't in here. Ned ran out of the restroom.

"Did you see a guy wearing tan Dockers and a red shirt come out of here?

"Hey, buddy, get lost, will you?" the guy said as he kissed the woman's neck.

Ned turned and started to walk away when the

young woman called out. "Hey, I watched him put some money into the 'bad date phone,'" she said, nodding toward the old payphone.

The young man stopped kissing her long enough to ask, "Bad date phone?"

"Yeah. If a girl finds her date is a little too 'touchy,' she excuses herself to go to the restroom Then she calls someone or a cab and never goes back to the guy. That's a bad date phone." She pointed to the phone on the wall.

"So, was that, like, what happened to you, mister?" The young guy laughed. "Maybe your boyfriend thought you were a bad date." Clearly, he'd had a bit too much to drink.

"Look, I'm not that way ... no, I was ... oh, don't worry about it," Ned said, flustered.

As he ran back to the bar, he looked at each table. The man was gone. Convinced that the man he'd just met was no longer there, Ned ran outside.

"He's gone!" he yelled out to the two officers who were getting out of their police cars.

"Are you the guy who called this in?" asked Officer Tom McHenry

"Yes. He was watching an unsolved crime show on the TV over the bar. A photo of the girl who was taken from the store flashed up on the screen. He said he'd had to tie her to the bed to get any. I went to the bathroom and called the police.

Officer McHenry interrupted. "Slow down. Just relax and take a deep breath."

Ned paused and took a breath. "The lady told me to try to keep him here. He went to the bathroom as I returned to my seat. I waited and tried to tell the bartender ... not sure if he understood. When I looked back at his seat, his duffle bag was gone, so I went back toward the men's room. A young couple was in the hallway. They told me he made a call on the payphone in the hallway after he came out of the men's room."

"What was he wearing?"

"He had on tan Dockers and a red shirt. Looked to be about in his twenties."

"Was he missing any front teeth? Did he have body odor?"

"No. I saw him smile. He had, you know, one of those bright white smiles. Like a movie star. No odor that I remember but the bar was pretty smelly."

"Did he mention what type of car he had, by any chance?" Officer McHenry asked.

"Bartender was going to cut him off about the time I sat down, and he told him he wasn't driving, so I assume he didn't have a vehicle."

"How tall would you guess him to be?"

"A little taller than me. I'm about five-eight. He

had one of those fancy hairstyles like you see on TV these days."

"Go over to that officer and give him a complete report." Officer Tom McHenry pointed to the other officer. "Hank, take a report. I'll go in and see if he's still in there. Oh ... and Hank, ask Jess to call the cab companies and see if they picked up anyone here at Moe's in the last thirty minutes. Someone saw him talking on the payphone. Maybe he called a cab to pick him up."

Colin positioned himself in the backseat of the cab so that he could see the passenger's side mirror. So far nothing. Probably the cops had been called to the bar for a rowdy drunk, he thought to himself. Then he saw it. Could it be? He looked a second time. Now he was sure of it. The flashing lights in the distance were from a police car, traveling in the same direction as the cab.

"Can you pull off the road? I think I'm going to be sick," Colin said.

The cabby pulled over on the side of Main Street.

"No, over in that alley, quick! I don't want everyone seeing me get sick," Colin said, pointing to an alleyway.

The cab driver made a sharp turn into the dark alley and turned off his lights to give his passenger more privacy. Colin stepped out, stuck one finger down his throat, and threw up. Just then, Colin felt a hand touch him on the shoulder. Out of instinct, he spun around and hit the driver in the face with his fist. The driver fell to the ground, unconscious. Colin then noticed that the driver was holding a wet towelette in his hands.

Colin looked at the driver, then kicked him in the head several times. He took the towelette out of the driver's hands, wiped his mouth, and tossed the towelette on the driver's body. Colin laughed as he left the driver's body in the alley, walked around to the open drivers-side door, and got behind the wheel.

Could someone have figured out who he was? He looked very different with his newly styled hair, tooth implants, and nice clothes. How could they? But he wasn't taking any chances. It was then that he heard the dispatcher asking everyone to radio in with their latest fares and locations.

The cab dispatcher did this at the request of the Lakewood Police. They didn't want to tip off the man they were after, and they hoped to not put the driver in any danger.

All of the cab drivers responded except the one who'd been dispatched to Moe's Bar. When that driver didn't respond, the dispatcher called his cell phone, which rang on the car's console. Colin did not answer it. Seeing a Kleenex box by the phone, he used a tissue to pick up the device, making sure his fingers never touched any part of the phone. He lowered the window and tossed out the phone as he drove by an empty field.

He decided to drive back to the airport. As he neared the large green overhead sign announcing Lakewood Airport, he saw several police cars along the exit. Quickly, he pulled the cab back into traffic. Colin drove, then stopped about a mile from the bus station.

He parked the car on a side road. Using several tissues, he wiped the taxi's steering wheel, gear shift, turn signal lever, and door handles. Then he picked up his duffle bag and walked the remaining distance to the bus station. Once inside, he scanned the overhead monitors for departing buses and times. It didn't matter where he went. His instincts told him to leave Lakewood and never return.

The next bus out wouldn't leave for another hour. Colin debated whether to wait or go back to the cab, drive out of Lakewood, and then take a flight from wherever he could get to. However, he knew he had to change clothes. He went into the men's room and splashed cold water on his face. Then he set the duffle bag on the counter and removed a brand-new white shirt and new jeans. After changing, he tossed the tan Dockers and red shirt into the trash. Through a crack in a stall door, a homeless man watched him.

Once he heard the door close, the homeless man pulled off his dirty, ragged shirt and pants and put on Colin's discarded clothes. He admired himself in the bathroom mirror. He turned on the faucet, washed his face, slicked back his hair, and smiled at his reflection. As he exited the men's room, the homeless man looked around at the passengers in the bus station. He didn't want to run into the man whose discarded clothes he'd taken from the trash.

He didn't see him anywhere. The homeless man slipped his hands into the pockets and felt something in the right-side one. In the man's haste to change, he had forgotten to empty his pockets. The homeless man pulled out five twenty-dollar bills, some loose change, and a piece of paper. That paper was a credit card receipt with the last four digits of an account number. It had been signed by Colin Bolton

CHAPTER 23

Connor's car skidded to a halt by the front door of Moe's Bar. He and Sundae jumped out.

"Where is he?" Connor asked, looking around and seeing only Officer Tom McHenry talking with another man.

"Gone," McHenry answered.

"How in the *hell*?" Connor yelled.

"Sir, from what we can tell, a cab picked him up. That's what we think, at least. The taxi company's dispatcher can't reach the cab driver. We have officers looking for the cab. Something must have tipped him off. This is Ned Ortiz. He's the gentleman who called in the tip. Do you want to question him?" McHenry asked.

"Transport him to the PD. Call Kate in and let

her question him. I'll start looking for the cab and driver," Connor said as he and Sundae headed for his car.

"The cab pulled out as we were pulling in and it was headed north," McHenry said. "Oh, and Connor, he's wearing tan Dockers pants and a red shirt. Also, Ned said he has all his teeth, not like we originally thought."

"We need a police sketch, if Ned can help us with that. Let Kate know, please," Connor said as he got back into his car.

Once Connor and Sundae were back in the vehicle, Connor heard a radio transmission from Officer Vince Brown of the Lakewood Police Department. The cab driver's cell phone had the GPS on. With the help of the cab dispatcher, he had located the phone in a field beside the highway. However, neither the cab nor the driver was with the phone.

"Where did you find it?" Connor asked.

"Old Airport Road," Vince radioed Connor.

"15, PD, do we have units at the airport?" Connor asked.

"Affirmative, we have units inside and out," the dispatcher replied.

"He either abducted the driver and cab or worse. Ask the cab dispatcher to get us a current photo of the cab driver and put out a BOLO for him. What about the Lakewood train and bus stations?" Connor asked.

"I'll request a photo of the cab driver from their dispatcher. Negative on the bus and train station. I'll get units over there right now. Be advised that Kate just came out of the interview room. The person who called in the tip said he saw an airline boarding pass in the man's duffle bag and copied down the name on it. Kate is calling airport security to see if she can get surveillance video and if the man by the name of Colin Bolton has another flight, or if Lakewood was his final destination," the Lakewood dispatcher reported.

Connor could hear the stress in Jessie's voice. She had been a dispatcher with the department for only a little over four months.

"If Lakewood airport security gets a video, have Kate show it to the person to see if he can ID the man. We'll need that video capture in a still format to get that out in a BOLO as well," Connor said. "I'll head over to the bus station. Call Bob and Grant and have them head over to the train station."

Connor pulled into the Lakewood bus station. As he and Sundae walked into the terminal, Connor's eyes scanned the lobby, seeking a security officer. When he didn't see one, he walked up to the ticket counter.

"I'm sorry, sir, but no dogs are allowed in here or on our buses," the ticket clerk said in a strong New York accent.

Connor pulled his badge from his belt and

showed it to the lady behind the counter. She blew a bubble with her chewing gum as she inspected Connor's ID.

"Well, no dogs are allowed," she said as she cracked her gum.

"This is a police dog. Now get me security!"

The clerk slowly picked up her phone and attempted to dial. Her fingernails were so long that Connor thought she should be cast in a horror film.

Finally, security arrived.

"That dog needs to be removed!" she said to the security officer.

Once again, Connor pulled his badge, then led the security officer away from the ticket window. Connor and the security officer split up searching the terminal.

"Son of a bit…!" Connor turned just in time to see a nun next to him and stopped midsentence.

Meeting back where they'd started, Connor and the security officer decided to check the front and back exteriors of the station.

Just as Connor and Sundae stepped outside, he saw a man sitting on a bench, eating from a bag.

"15, PD, outside Lakewood Bus station. I have a male who is wearing what looks like Dockers and a red shirt."

"10-4."

Connor approached the man from the side and motioned for Sundae to approach from the opposite side, in case the subject ran. Slowly, both Connor and Sundae approached the bench from opposite sides.

"Sir, may I have an ID, please?"

"I … don't have … one," stammered the homeless man.

"What is your name?" Connor asked.

"Carl…"

"Carl what?"

"Carl Bennett." The homeless man swallowed hard.

"Carl, do you have any ID at all on you?"

"No." Thinking he was in trouble for taking the clothes on his back, Carl stood and bolted.

He made it only about five feet before Sundae grabbed his pant leg and he was on the ground. Connor was right behind them and stood Carl up.

"Let's go to the Lakewood Police Department and have a talk. Carl, if that's your name, why did you run?" Connor asked as he patted the man down. Connor heard a crinkling sound in the man's left pocket. "What's this?" he asked as he pulled out the credit card receipt with Colin Bolton's name. Connor cuffed the man and started for his car to take the man in.

"I can explain. These aren't my clothes. Really," Carl said from the backseat of Connor's car.

"PD, be advised that I am en route to the PD. I have a subject who tells me that his name is Carl

Bennett. However, I found a credit card receipt on him with the name Colin Bolton. We'll need the man Kate is interviewing to ID him."

Then Connor turned around. "What do you mean, they aren't your clothes?" he asked.

CHAPTER 24

Connor slammed on the brakes, then pulled over to the shoulder of the highway and opened the back door of his car.

"Tell me! What the hell do you mean, those aren't your clothes?" he asked impatiently.

"I was in the men's bathroom in a stall. I'm sort of homeless at this time. See, if I'm in a stall, they can't toss me out of the lobby. This man came into the bathroom, carrying a duffle bag. He washed his face, then used the restroom. Then he came back to his duffle bag, which he set on the sink," Carl said, shook up.

"So, you're telling me you took the clothes off this guy?"

"No, I peeked out and watched him through the crack between the wall and the stall door."

"And?" Connor prodded.

"He took off his shirt and pants and tossed them into the trash. They looked brand-new. When he left the bathroom, I came out of the stall and tried on the clothes. They fit. I found the receipt and five twenties in the pocket. I got something to eat with the money. That was what I was doing when you found me. That's all ... really."

Connor got back in the driver's seat, turned the car around, and parked in the bus station parking lot.

"Tell me what he looked like and what clothes he put on."

"He pulled on a pair of new blue jeans and a new white shirt."

"How do you know they were new?" Connor asked.

"I saw him pull the tags off the shirt. When the one from the jeans wouldn't come off, he used his teeth."

"15, PD, I need a unit at the Lakewood bus station ASAP."

To Carl, Connor said, "Okay, show me where this trash can is." He opened the back door and helped the man out of the car. Sundae walked alongside them.

Inside, Connor opened the men's room door on the left side of the terminal door and they walked in.

"There," the homeless man pointed with his shoulder, as he was still in handcuffs. Connor walked over to the trashcan and pulled out some old, dirty clothes.

"These yours?" Connor held them up.

"Yes."

Then Connor saw the discarded clothes tags, beneath where the clothes had been. From his pocket, he pulled out a pair of latex gloves. Then he pulled a paper towel from the dispenser and grabbed the two tags from the trashcan.

"Did he put anything else in here?"

"No, I only saw him drop the pants and shirt in the trash. Now, can I put his clothes back and put mine on?" Carl asked

"No. I want to know why you ran. I have a unit coming to take you to the police station. I want you to tell them everything you can remember about the man you saw in here."

Connor removed the cuffs as the Lakewood unit pulled into the parking lot. Connor explained what he had been told. He asked the officers to print the man first to make sure he wasn't wanted for anything. Then Carl was to give a complete report to Kate as to how he'd gotten the clothes. "Also, have the guy who called from the bar take a good look at him to make sure," Connor concluded.

Next, Connor radioed the Lakewood dispatcher with the latest on the clothes change and asked if they had found out anything about the name that Ned had seen on the boarding pass. Connor looked around the bus station, convinced that if what the homeless man had told him was correct, Colin Bolton was not there anymore. That left only the train station.

After three hours of intensive searching at the airport, bus station, and train depot, nothing else had turned up. Connor and Sundae returned to the police department. Kate told him that Ned had confirmed that the clothes on Carl, the homeless man, were correct. However, Carl wasn't the man Ned had seen at the bar. Kate had situated both men in separate interview rooms and had food and drink delivered to both.

"I have nineteen Colin Boltons who live in the state," Kate said. "Only one lives in the Lakewood area. I sent a unit to the address, but no one was home. I have the others turned into their local PDs to see what they can find out."

"The one here in Lakewood—is it a rental or does the person own the place?" Connor asked.

"No clue. Once it gets later in the morning, we can drive over there and talk to the neighbors. We have only about an hour; let's get something to eat," Kate suggested.

Connor pulled the paper towel and another pair of latex gloves from his pocket and set the tags on the desk.

"Oh, gee, you shouldn't have. They're not my

size." Kate laughed as she looked at the clothes tags. "Or my style."

"I'll run this downstairs and ask our CSI team to do their magic. Carl said he bit the tag off the jeans. Should be some DNA left on the tag. I know you sent the team over to the men's room but I was afraid of someone coming in the restroom and, well, you know.

"Okay. I'll get some breakfast sent up here," Kate said

"Stay," Connor said to Sundae as she curled up in her bed beside Connor's desk.

Kate ordered pancakes and coffee, then went to Connor's desk. She took out Sundae's bowls and gave her kibble and fresh water.

Sundae looked up from her empty bowl as the elevator dinged and Connor stepped off. He looked around but didn't see Kate.

"I'm sorry. I should have fed you before I left," Connor said to Sundae as she watched him pour another helping into her bowl. He was putting the bag back while Sundae made short order of the kibble in her bowl when Kate came out carrying the breakfast. The office filled with the warm aroma of pancakes and bacon.

"No, don't feed her!" Kate said as Connor held the bag midair.

"I just did."

"I fed her before I went down to get our breakfast."

Sundae stepped back, smelling their breakfast with her nose at their desks.

"You little con artist!" Connor said, looking down at Sundae.

Sundae, who wasn't at all ashamed about having gotten two breakfasts out of Kate and Connor, was now negotiating for them to share theirs with her.

After she took her last sip of coffee, Kate looked up at the clock. "Let's go by that address for the Colin Bolton in Lakewood," she said.

Just then, her phone rang. From the one-sided conversation, Connor surmised it must have been Theo Atwell. He motioned that he would be at the front desk. Connor talked to the dispatcher until Kate appeared. Despite having been awake for most of the night, she still looked amazing, he thought to himself.

"That was Eric from CSI. They pulled prints off the clothes tags and ran a rapid DNA test off the tag he bit."

"And?" Connor asked as they walked out to the parking lot.

"Nothing on file. He'll send the tags into the crime lab for more testing.

Connor was about to turn the car off Main Street when they received a call that the cab driver had been found in an alley and was being transported to

Lakewood Hospital. Connor waited for an opening in the oncoming traffic, then made a U-turn to go to the hospital.

"Drop me off at the PD. I'll go talk to the cab driver," Kate said. "You check out the neighborhood and see if that's the Colin we're looking for."

Connor thought about it and decided that Kate was right. This way, they could cover more ground at once. He stopped at the PD and Kate jumped out. As he pulled away from the curb, she heard him call into the PD that he was en route to 24 Trixie Lane.

CHAPTER 25

Connor pulled into the driveway at 24 Trixie Lane and glanced down at the wrinkled piece of paper on which Kate had written the address, to make sure he was in the correct place. He didn't know what he'd expected Colin Bolin to live in, but whatever it was, this was not it.

The old blue and white mobile home was the one where Sundae had run to and at whose back she had barked. At the time, Connor and Kate had thought she was barking at the neighbor's cat. Connor opened his car door. Sundae jumped over the seat and scampered to Connor's left side. He unsnapped his holster, then bent down to Sundae and gave the alert command. She knew that this meant the house may be an unsafe place and that she should be careful and alert.

The lawn was overgrown with weeds and littered

with leaves and trash. It looked as though no one had been there or cared about the appearance of where they lived for quite some time—or maybe both. Connor remembered that all the windows at this trailer house had been covered with aluminum foil. He stepped up onto the porch and knocked. No one answered the door, so he knocked a second time.

"Lakewood Police, open up!"

Still, no one came to the door. As he looked at the windows from the porch, he heard a voice.

"He ain't there."

Connor spun around.

"Haven't seen him in probably a few weeks," said a woman as Connor stepped down off the porch.

"And you would be?" Connor asked.

"I should ask the same of you. Why are you snooping around this place?"

The woman's voice was as stern as a master sergeant. Her hair was coarse, the color of straw, and looked like a used Brillo pad. Connor could tell this woman was gruff as hell. He wondered if possibly she could be Annie Oakley reincarnated. Give her a holster with two six-guns strapped on and she would be the total package.

"Detective Connor Maxwell." Connor took another step closer.

"Got some ID on you, Mister Detective?"

Connor pulled his badge case off his belt. He first

showed the front of the badge, then turned it to the back with his ID card. The woman pulled it from his hand and studied the photo, then squinted up at him, comparing the photo to his face.

"Awfully pretty for a detective, Detective."

Connor was unsure what to say to that. Was that a compliment or an insult?

"You next," Connor said.

"Name's Dottie. Dottie Westbrook. What can I do you for, Detective?" Dottie kept a discerning eye on Connor as she handed him his badge case.

"I'm looking for Colin Bolton. This is the address we found on file for him."

"Like I said, he ain't been here for weeks. You should call Mr. Noble. He rents out this place. The lady who lived here before was a right nice young lady but this guy, he was spooky-looking. Odd bird, I'd say."

"Do you have Mr. Noble's phone number? Connor asked.

"Do I look like a phone book, Detective Maxwell?"

Connor almost burst out laughing but thought better of it. "No, ma'am, you don't. I'll look it up and call him. Thank you for your help."

Connor and Sundae returned to their car. Although Ms. Dottie Westbrook went back to tending and watering her bushes, she never took her eyes off Connor.

"15, PD, can you see if you can find a phone number for a Mr. Noble in Lakewood?"

"Will do. Everything okay over there?" asked Sandy Curtis, the dispatcher.

"I think I may have run into Annie Oakley."

"Repeat?" Sandy said.

"Nothing, lack of sleep. I just need a phone number if you can find one for Noble."

Several minutes of radio silence passed before the radio crackled.

"Free to copy?" Sandy asked.

"Go ahead," Connor said as he watched Dottie Westbrook move closer to hear what he was saying. Connor raised his window.

"There is a Roger Noble, and I'm sorry to say, he is the only Noble listed in Lakewood. Hope he's the one you're looking for."

Sandy gave him the phone number and Connor quickly dialed it. He told Mr. Noble who he was and that he would like to have access to the home of Colin Bolton on Trixie Drive.

The elderly voice of Mr. Noble was as stern and no-nonsense as that of Dottie Westbrook. He informed Connor that he would need a search warrant before he would unlock Mr. Bolton's door for him. Mr. Noble didn't care who Connor was. Without the proper paperwork, there would be no access.

"15, PD, is Kate back from the hospital yet?"

"No, she's still there," Sandy said.

"How about Bob or Grant?"

"Yes, both are right here with me."

"Ask Bob and Grant if they can get me a search warrant ASAP from Judge Gilmore for Colin Bolton's mobile home at 24 Trixie Lane. I'll stay here unless there's an issue getting the judge to sign off on it."

"By the way," Sandy said. "Just an FYI. Candy Martin and a few other reporters are parked in the parking lot."

"Wonderful," Connor said.

"Like a pack of hungry wolves."

Kate sat in the ER lobby of Lakewood Hospital. Every thirty minutes, the doctor or nurse gave her updates on their patient, the cab driver. Thus far, the man had not woken up. Kate had learned that the cab driver's name was Armand Patel. He was forty years old and had a wife and four children. She prayed that he would make it for his family's sake, but she also desperately needed to talk to him to see if he could remember anything about Colin Bolton. Kate texted the information she had found out about the cabbie to Connor and to the department.

"Detective, Stroup," a female voice called out.

DANCING QUEEN

Kate looked up to see the nurse. She quickly stood and hurried to the ER doors.

"Yes?" Kate said.

"Mr. Patel is awake. The doctor said he will allow you only five minutes—no longer."

The nurse opened the ER door for Kate. The cab driver's eyes were swollen and he had a palette of red, blue, and black bruises on his face and neck. These were due to the kicks that Colin had delivered to him once he was on the ground.

"Mr. Patel, my name is Kate Stroup. I'm a detective with the Lakewood Police Department. Are you able to tell us anything about the man who beat you last night after you picked him up?"

CHAPTER 26

Bob and Grant pulled in behind Connor's car with a signed search warrant in hand. They had first delivered a copy to Mr. Noble, who was now also pulled to a stop at the curbside. Noble, a man in his late seventies, with wispy white hair, stepped out of an old Ford truck, shaking the stiffness out of his legs from the short ten-minute drive over.

Connor introduced himself.

Dottie Westbrook was beside herself with all the action unfolding right next door to her house. She waved to Mr. Noble and gave a "woo-hoo." Mr. Noble ambled forward with keys in hand, not paying Dottie the least bit of attention. Connor swore he heard her say, "You old coot." Connor thought Noble was a smart man. He'd probably put two and two together and figured that old Dottie was seeking the scoop about what was going on next door. Noble was like a fish that just wouldn't bite. He kept his distance from her.

Mr. Noble unlocked the trailer door without opening it and then stepped back, allowing Connor, Bob, and Grant to enter. While they put on paper booties and gloves, Mr. Noble yelled to them as he stepped off the porch that he had left the key in the lock and would be leaving.

"Oh, my God!" Connor said as he took a step into the house. By then, the odor had wafted out to the porch.

"Let me get the Vicks from our unit," Bob said as he ran to his car.

All three detectives put Vicks under their noses and Connor locked Sundae in his car. The three detectives entered the trailer. Connor thought the house smelled like a combination of human waste and trash. Taking in the home's interior, they saw that the place was a mess. The trash can was overflowing with half-eaten food, while more containers were scattered across the floor. It was obvious, Connor thought to himself, that Colin had never taken any lessons on home décor from Martha Stewart

"So glad he knew we were coming and straightened up for us," Connor said.

Bob had found a large pile of porn magazines on the old kitchen table. Connor walked over to the table and saw a red light blinking—barely visible and peeking through one of the stacks. Gently, he pushed the stack to the side and found an answering machine.

"Looks like Colin has some messages," Grant said.

Satisfied that they had sufficiently looked at the living area, the detectives walked down a long hallway, where the smell got worse. The hall bathroom was as filthy as the front room, with unwashed towels and heaps of dirty clothes. Connor tried to find a light switch for the hallway but couldn't. The three men used their Maglites as the sunlight from the front door dissipated the farther they walked down the hall.

Grant's shoe caught on something in the hall. He looked down, saw a pair of jockey shorts, and shook them off the toe of his shoe.

Connor felt around a dark bedroom wall for a light switch. The room filled with light. "Holy shit," he said.

"This is our guy," Bob said as the three stepped carefully into the back bedroom.

A trash can stood against the wall, filled with what appeared to be, and smelled like, human fecal matter and urine. About eighteen inches of rope had been tied to each of the four legs of the bed

"I'm sure this is where he held her," Connor said.

On the other side of the bed, a pile of woman's clothes lay on the floor. Connor noticed that the clothes appeared to have been ripped or cut from her body.

"I'll go put up the crime scene tape," Grant said, turning to Connor.

"Oh, Grant, be careful. The lady next door is a cross between a barracuda and wild cat," Connor said, jokingly.

To Bob, he said, "Let's all clear out. I'll call the CSI team to get over here. Can you get a uniform patrolman over here to guard the crime scene until CSI clears it?"

"Connor, it may take them hours to go through all this. Does this trailer still have axles and wheels under it? If it does, I think the PD could get them to pull it over, to process the mobile home easier," Bob said.

"Not sure Noble would allow it and if the DA would want the home removed," Connor said.

"You better let the CSI boys know this isn't a five-star," Bob said.

Connor went out to his unit and retrieved a paper bag from the trunk. He took it inside and retrieved a man's tee-shirt, which he'd seen on the bathroom floor. He'd need this for Sundae to pick up Colin's scent if they ended up tracking him.

As he stepped out of the mobile home, Connor

saw a news van turning on to Trixie Lane. He knew that, within minutes, there would be more reporters swarming around the crime scene tape than bees at a hive.

Connor took the paper bag and put it in his trunk, then unlocked the door so Sundae could follow him. He had to question Dottie Westbrook, so he walked next door, leaving Bob and Grant to deal with the press.

Dottie had made herself comfortable in a lawn chair and was holding a tall glass of iced tea as she watched the crime scene unfold before her eyes. She couldn't wait for lunchtime at the senior center so that she could tell all her friends about what was going on right next door.

Connor opened Dottie's front gate and walked over to her. "Do you think we could talk?" he asked.

"Well, it seems you're talking, Detective."

Connor removed a photo of Lacey from his sport coat and handed it to Dottie. "Do you remember seeing this woman with Colin Bolton? You seem very observant of the neighborhood activity."

Dottie remained seated in her lawn chair, the photo in one hand and her iced tea in the other. She studied the picture.

"No, Detective Maxwell. I can't say I ever saw her over there. I did, however, see her photo on TV when she went missing. Before that, I would get my gas at Joe's. She was a nice young girl, very sweet.'

"You never heard screaming or any noise coming from the trailer?"

"No, I didn't. The man living over there was odd. He was always walking everywhere. I'd see him walking down Main Street many times, always alone. He wasn't a looker ... you know, with those missing front teeth and never bathing. I tell you, I could smell him when he walked past my house if the wind was just right."

"Was the foil always on the windows next door?"

"No, not until he moved in. Not sure why he put foil over the windows. He would leave early in the evenings. Never was sure when he came back."

"Did he work?" Connor asked.

"Now, detective, I have no idea if the man was employed or not. Maybe that's where he walked off to each night. I do know that when he rented the place, Noble told me someone from Boston paid a year's rent in advance."

"Boston. Hmm." Connor pulled a business card out of his wallet and gave it to Dottie. "That has the number to the police department and my cell phone number on it. If you think of anything, anything at all, call us. We'll have a uniformed officer here until we clear the scene."

"Oh, there is one thing I almost forgot. I think he bought himself a new Ford truck. You know, one of those fancy, shiny things with more chrome on them."

"Truck?"

"Yes. He brought it home and it was in the drive, right there." She pointed up close to the porch. "The next thing I knew, it was gone and I never saw him after that. I thought maybe he moved or took a vacation."

CHAPTER 27

At first, Connor was speechless. His mind reeled with everything Dottie had just said. At the mention of a new truck, or what appeared to be a new truck, Connor's thoughts turned to Cody. He'd had his 2019 Ford truck taken from Moe's bar the day he'd gotten drunk and called his sister to drive him home. The truck did have DNA from Lacey. Connor wondered if Colin used the truck to move Lacey while she was alive—or to move her dead body. Colin had taken her car the morning of the abduction, but it was later found abandoned. They hadn't found a body in the mobile home. Did Colin have her tied up someplace else?

"Do you remember how long the truck was here?"

"I saw it over there only once," Dottie said, taking a swig from her iced tea. "Then he was gone and I never saw anyone over there until you and the cavalry showed up here this morning."

Connor chuckled at her description of the action next door. He pulled out his phone and banged out a quick message to Sandy at the PD, requesting a photo of Cody's truck. Photos had been taken by the CSI team. Within a few minutes, his phone dinged. He opened the message and saw a picture of Cody's Ford truck.

He held out his phone. "Ms. Westbrook, is this the truck you saw next door?"

"Yep! That's it," Dottie said, pointing a finger at Connor's phone.

Though Bob and Grant were right next door, Connor knew that texting them and Kate would keep this piece of information out of the media, at least for the moment.

The CSI van rolled to a rumbling stop as Bob and Grant made the media vans move farther down the street. Connor thanked Dottie. Then he and Bob moved their units so that the CSI van could get as close to the house as possible.

It was just about lunchtime, so Dottie headed out to the senior center, excited to share her newfound information. She pulled out of the driveway with a broad smile across her face. She knew she would be the hit of the senior center, at least for today.

Connor, Bob, and Grant met with the CSI team for a few minutes until a uniformed Lakewood officer came to stand guard over the home until CSI released the place.

It had been twenty-four hours since Colin had last been seen. Kate and Connor had been summoned downstairs to meet with Eric Martinez, the CSI lead tech.

Eric had set the dirty answering machine on a table.

"Disgusting! Didn't this guy ever wash his hands?" Kate asked as she looked at the machine.

Eric chuckled and raised his gloved hand. "There's more than one reason why I use these," he said as he moved closer to the machine. "Connor, you saw that there were five new messages on the red digital display the day you were in the mobile home. It seems like this dude never erased any messages. Here is a transcription of all the messages for you." Eric handed the document to Connor. "But listen to this message." Eric pressed play on the machine.

"Colin, this is Dad. I haven't heard from you in weeks. If I don't hear something soon, I'm flying in from Boston. You're giving me no choice."

Eric pressed stop.

"I called a buddy of mine to get the phone records from this landline. Other than telemarketers, the only calls coming in are from the same number. It belongs to an Edward A. Bolton. I can assume this is his father," Eric said.

"Thanks, Eric," Connor said as they turned to leave.

"Oh, one other thing," Eric said. "We're still processing the scene. When I was looking over that back bedroom in the mobile home, I found a pile of women's clothes that had been literally ripped off of her. Next to them, I found a woman's fingernail. She must have struggled. The DNA was a match to both Lacey and Colin. The one sheet that was left beside the bed had both their DNA on it as well.

"I have more things that I'm processing in our lab and some that I sent off to the FBI. Lastly, nothing comes back on his fingerprints, so we can assume that he has no previous record or hasn't ever been caught."

"I have a really hard time believing that."

"Even our profiler feels certain that this wasn't his first time. Remember what she told us in her report?" Kate said, looking at Connor.

They walked out into the hall, where Connor leaned his head and one leg against the wall.

"I'm tired, Kate," he said with a heavy sigh.

"We haven't had a lot of sleep in the last few days," she said. As she brushed a lock of hair from his forehead, she noticed that his eyes were moist.

"No. I'm tired of always being reactive and not

proactive. I took this job to make a difference. By the time we get the case, nine times out of ten, it's too late. Someone is dead or dying while we're chasing some dirtbag. I just don't want to give another family the news that their daughter or son is not coming home alive."

Connor's downcast look made Kate want to hold and comfort him. Instead, she said, "Come on. We need to get back to the office so we can call this Edward Bolton."

"I think we need a flight to Boston. Screw calling. Colin is probably there as we speak."

Connor made arrangements for Sundae to stay with Bob and his wife, Bettie Jo, while he and Kate were in Boston. He knew that Sundae could ride along with Bob and Grant during the day and spend the evenings with Bob and his wife.

Kate put in the request to fly to Boston. As soon as it was approved, she made flight arrangements for the two of them to leave the next day. Their flight had a layover in Dallas and touched down at Logan International Airport a few minutes before midnight.

The media was now flashing around a grainy airport photo of Colin. The media had dubbed him "Colin the Chameleon." Some people had described him as dirty, poorly dressed, and without front teeth. Others said he was well-dressed, with a stylish haircut and bright white smile. Connor hated when the media gave someone like Colin a nickname, glorifying the person rather than focusing on his crimes.

Colin found a hotel for the night. He left his bag on the bed and went down to the lobby. Then he got back in the cab and drove until he found a self-service car wash. At that hour of the evening, no one was there. He opened the car, turned on the soap, and washed the interior of the cab, then the exterior. Assuming no one had found the cab driver, maybe those red lights he'd seen on the night he took the cab meant nothing. Once he felt that the car was clean, he abandoned it at the car wash.

Colin walked to a mall. With the cash he had stolen from the cab driver before leaving him for dead, he purchased two new shirts and pairs of slacks. Colin ate at the food court, where he couldn't keep his eyes off a young couple making out. She was a pretty woman with light brown hair and big eyes.

CHAPTER 28

*E*dward Bolton sat comfortably on a large, luxurious leather couch, his feet propped up on a matching ottoman in his lavishly furnished den. He was enjoying his new 110-inch flat-screen Ultra HDTV, which hung from the wall. With the remote in hand, he flipped through the channels while adjusting the volume. Suddenly, an image caught his eye as he flipped to the next channel. Quickly, Edward directed the remote back to the previous channel.

It was the tail end of a national news segment. The newscaster was talking about the male suspect shown in the on-screen photo. The sight of the man and the name under the photo made Edward catch his breath and caused his heart to sink.

"Oh my God," Edward said out loud.

"Anyone knowing the whereabouts of this man is

asked to call police immediately. He should be considered dangerous," the newsman said, warning the public.

Edward Bolton sat stunned, paralyzed by what he was seeing. The photo on the television was of his son Colin. While the image was grainy, he was able to make out his son's features—plus, the authorities had Colin's name. What had he done this time? The word "dangerous" kept echoing in his mind. Edward felt sick to his stomach. He had been calling Colin over the last few weeks, with no answer or return phone call.

Surely the news report was a mistake; it had to be. Edward had to know what Colin was being accused of doing, then call his attorney. Looking at his watch, he saw that it was late, but his attorney would surely take his call. Edward picked up the remote, which had slid from his hand, and began flipping through all the channels. Finally, he found an all-news channel. While he waited, watching a segment on some university, Edward felt his blood pressure rising with each minute. He checked the app on his wristwatch and saw that the digital readout was through the roof. He reached over to an oak end table for his blood pressure medication and a glass of wine and downed them.

Shortly after a report on global warming, the same grainy photo of Colin appeared on the screen. "Authorities are looking for this man, Colin A.

Bolton, seen in the photo on your screen. He was last seen in Lakewood, New Mexico. Authorities have been searching for him in connection with the disappearance of a young woman, Lacey Warner. Warner was abducted a month and a half ago from a convenience store in Lakewood. She is the mother of three young children. DNA from Warner and Bolton has been found at Bolton's residence in Lakewood. Bolton is also sought for the abduction of a cab driver in the Lakewood area. The cab driver was badly beaten and the cab stolen. The cab driver is in grave condition at Lakewood Memorial Hospital."

Edward thought about how the newscaster moved on to the next story as if it were just another day in broadcast land. Then Edward picked up his cell phone and hit the speed dial for his attorney. The call went directly to voicemail, and Edward felt his pulse racing. His lawyer always took his calls, no matter what time of the day or night it was. Nonetheless, Edward left a brief message, stating that it was urgent and to call him back as soon as possible. Several hours passed as he sat silently in his den, his mind racing like a roller coaster, out of control.

Hours later and with no call from his attorney, Edward retired to his bedroom. Sleep eluded him as he tossed and turned until he finally got up. He tried to wrap his brain around how and why Colin would have done this. He remembered his attorney giving Edward a stern warning that Colin was escalating his lewd behavior. The attorney's advice had been to show tough love to the young man and stop bailing him out each time he got into trouble. That was after the second time Colin had been accused of rape. Edward had paid the victims anonymously through his attorney. It had been guilt money for what his son had done to the woman and young girl. After each payment, Edward realized that no amount of money could ever take away the lifetime of pain or the scars of those victims whom Colin had left behind.

The attorney had gotten not one, but two, judges to sentence Colin to a mental hospital to rehabilitate the young man. Edward wondered if his attorney had already seen the television coverage and decided to wash his hands of both Edward and Colin. Was that why he hadn't returned Edward's call?

Edward was still mulling over these events the following morning. The doorbell interrupted his thoughts. Edward opened the door to find a young man and woman in his courtyard.

"Edward A. Bolton?" the young man said.

Edward, looking down, noticed that the man wore black Western boots, which was odd footwear for the Boston area.

"I'm Edward. What can I help you with?"

"I'm Detective Connor Maxwell and this is my partner, Detective Kate Stroup. We would like to ask you a few questions about your son, Colin."

After what he'd seen on TV the previous night, Edward realized that he shouldn't be surprised that detectives would show up on his doorstep

"Would you both like to come in? I can have tea or coffee brought out to the deck," Edward said.

"It doesn't matter," Kate said, so Edward ushered them into his den.

Connor and Kate observed the lavish furnishings. Connor recalled the filthy mobile home with overflowing trash cans, dirty clothes on the floor, and the overpowering stench that had required the detectives to use Vicks under their noses to even get through the door. The two homes stood in stark contrast to each other.

"Mr. Bolton, your son…"

Edward interrupted Connor.

"I saw a segment on the news last night. I had no idea. I have called Colin several times over the past few weeks, but he didn't answer or call me back."

"Mr. Bolton, have you heard from Colin at all?" Kate asked.

"No."

"When is the last time you spoke to him?" Connor asked.

"It has been about two months, I think." Edward considered the question. "Yes, about two months."

"Mr. Bolton, has Colin ever shown any violent behavior or done anything like this before?" Connor asked.

Edward thought about the question. Should he tell them now about what had happened in the past? Should he say, "I want an attorney"? Or did that make him sound like he was guilty? Edward wished his attorney had called him back; he surely would have advised him as to what to say.

CHAPTER 29

Connor and Kate returned to their hotel rooms after meeting with Edward. Their return flight wasn't until the next morning, so they decided to do some sight-seeing. They freshened up and went to Faneuil Hall, where they found a place that specialized in chocolate chip cookies. Connor purchased a bag and they ate while walking. They talked about the Lacey Warner case and window-shopped. Later, they walked by the Salty Dog, where a mixture of delicious smells caught their attention.

"I'm hungry. How about you?" Connor asked.

Kate grabbed his hand and they went inside.

After the waiter took their order, Connor looked across the table at Kate. He thought she had never looked as beautiful as she did now.

"Can we talk?" Connor asked.

"Yes. You have me worried. What's on your mind?"

"The other day, you asked about us, just before Candy Martin and her microphone interrupted us. I thought we could talk about that."

Connor waited for Kate to say something, but she didn't, so he continued.

"Anyway, I guess you're seeing other people. The rumor mill at the PD had you out with one of the sheriff's deputies. Then, the other night, Carlos and I ran into you and Theo. So, when you asked me that, I figured you had moved on."

"Connor, Theo was the one who checked into getting access to the state police pilot with the drone for us. I'll admit, he's eye candy for the ladies. However, it's been my experience that men like that slip their leash. I know, it sounds like I'm putting all men like him into one category. Honestly, I end up comparing all men to you. I fell in love with you…"

"But…?" Connor asked as the waiter set two large, steaming plates of seafood in front of them, along with hot rolls and butter.

"Will there be anything else, sir?" the waiter asked

"No, thank you," Connor replied.

The waiter removed their salad plates and then left the table.

"Connor, the 'but' has to do with our work. We both felt that the closer we got, the harder it was to perform our duties. We don't just work in an office. Sometimes we're put in life-and-death situations. That's why we originally decided to put some space between us."

"But does that space minimize the love we both feel?"

"Honestly, no, but where do we go from here?" Kate looked at Connor for an answer.

"I wasn't going to say anything until I knew whether or not I was accepted, but I've applied for a position with the FBI. If I were working with the feds and you with Lakewood PD, we'd no longer be working together."

Kate swallowed and thought about what Connor had just said. "The FBI?"

"Yes."

At Logan International Airport, Connor and Kate stood up to get in the security line. Just as Connor bent over to pick up their overnight bags, they each received a text message from Bob. The message read, "Cab was located in Tulsa, OK, found abandoned in a car wash bay. Both inside and outside have been washed like Cody Lambert's truck. Lakewood will be sending for it. CSI will look it over. Checked with TSA. No passengers by the name of Colin Bolton on any passenger list. Notified both bus and train stations in the Tulsa area. Negative on anyone by that name on their lists. Sent photo in case he was able to get a fake ID. Oh, BTW, Connor—Bettie and I woke up this morning to find Sundae in bed with us. Think she is missing you. Bob."

Connor sat back down and quickly replied to Bob's text. "Would you or Sandy check with car rentals? Give Tulsa PD his photo and check with any stolen vehicles after the cab was dropped off. Ask TPD to post the photo around truck stops in case he tries to hitch a ride out of town. We are boarding our flight, will check text messages on our next layover in Dallas."

"He's heading east," Connor told Kate.

"I just hope his father will do the right thing and call the Boson PD to pick him up if he does show up there," Kate said.

"One can only hope."

"Did you notice that when we asked if Colin had ever been in trouble before, Edward hesitated before saying no?" Kate asked as they walked toward the security checkpoint.

"Yes. His dad has the money to buy a lot of things. But, would a father buy his son out of a jam? I know my dad and mom wouldn't," Connor said.

Edward paced across the deck, remembering the photos that Detective Maxwell had showed him of ropes tied to the bed, the stacks of porn magazines on the table, and the filth Maxwell had described to him. Edward's attorney hadn't returned his call. Nonetheless, as he thought about the young woman and her children, Edward knew that he had to tell them about Colin's past—with or without his attorney. He had to do the right thing, even if his son didn't.

Edward grabbed his cell phone off the patio table and called the number on Connor's business card. The phone rang twice, then went to voice mail. Looking at his watch, he remembered that the two detectives were catching a flight out of Logan. Edward assumed that he had missed them.

"Detective Maxwell, this is Edward Bolton. I need to talk to you as soon as possible. Please give me a call, no matter what time you get this message."

Edward felt better after leaving the message. He knew in his heart that neither money nor a good attorney would change Colin. It was far beyond that now. No matter what, Edward blamed himself for Colin's behavior. He had enrolled Colin in the best schools that money could buy, but Colin still got in trouble. Maybe things would have been different if Colin's mother had stayed in the marriage. She had been afraid of the child's behavioral issues back in grade school.

Colin had been caught in the girls' bathroom. Then he had inappropriately touched a teacher. Mary had been brought up in a staunch Catholic home, as had Edward. However, when Colin had once again been caught in the girls' bathroom, school counselors advised that the boy needed more than just a scolding. He needed professional help. Edward refused.

Mary left and, although it was against her religious beliefs, she filed for divorce several months later. She felt that Colin was emotionally unstable, and no matter how she tried, she couldn't get Edward to stop bailing him out of trouble with his money. A year after their divorce, Mary passed away from cancer. Edward could still hear Mary's pleading words. Now he wished that he had listened to her.

Edward had such high hopes for his son when he was born, giving him his father's first name and his own middle name. He truly felt that someday Colin would work with him in the family business, get married, and have children of his own.

"A father's dream for his son," Edward said aloud as a tear rolled down his cheek and fell to the flagstone between his feet. This was followed by another tear until Edward put both hands to his face and sobbed deeply. The live-in housekeeper heard his cries and walked onto the porch. She sat on the loveseat and put her arms around Edward to comfort him.

"Mr. Bolton," she said after a moment, "there is a call for you on the home phone from a Detective Maxwell. Do you want me to bring the phone to you or do you wish to call him back?"

"Please, bring the phone to me," Edward said as he tried to compose himself.

CHAPTER 30

Colin kept eyeing the young couple in the food court. The woman attracted his attention. She was a pretty, petite blonde with bright blue eyes. He overheard her ask for a refill of her drink. The young man refused, telling her that he'd spent the last of his money on their meal. Colin walked over and placed a twenty-dollar bill on their table.

"For the lady's drink." Colin flashed his brand-new implant smile at the woman and then returned to his table.

He heard the young man's voice rise. Clearly, he wasn't happy about accepting money from a stranger, especially a man.

The girl got up and ordered herself another drink. She put the remainder of the twenty in the pocket of her tight jeans before glancing at Colin and winking. Colin smiled back, then looked over at the young man. He hoped that the guy would leave the girl and that she would come over to Colin. He watched as the woman returned to their table, and noticed that she kept looking over at him.

Nice clothes, a new smile, and a hundred-dollar haircut could do a lot, he thought to himself. Now, if only he knew how to talk to a woman, the way men did in the movies. Clearly, she was interested in him. But he still had to get back to Boston.

Colin had dumped the cab the previous night. He was afraid that air travel would be too risky if the cabbie had described him to the police. That was when he had formulated a plan but he was unsure whether it would work.

He walked back to the couple's table. "Excuse me. I'm trying to get back to Boston. My car broke down and I was wondering if you could give me a lift to the edge of town. Then maybe I could catch a ride on the freeway."

"You got enough money to buy my girl a large Coke. Why don't you just go buy an airline ticket, buddy?" the young man asked.

"Walt, that's no way to talk to someone!"

"Fear of flying," Colin lied to the young man.

"Get lost!" Walt said.

Colin stood there a moment longer, then turned and walked away. The young couple stood up. Walt grabbed the girl's arm and they left.

Colin thought about hiring another cab driver

but was worried. If the cabbie had lived, then Colin's face would be all over the news. He thought about Lacey and decided that they would never put those two things together. He had forgotten how drunk he had been in Moe's Bar that night and he didn't realize what he'd said to the stranger sitting next to him. So many beers had made him more talkative than usual.

He turned one last time to see whether the young lady had turned around. She hadn't. Colin finished his drink and then stood up when he saw a mall cop. Quickly, Colin put his head down and walked away. He needed another car or a ride.

"Trying to pick up that pretty young thing, were you?" a lady's voice asked behind him.

He turned to find a woman about ten years his senior, standing and smiling at him.

"No, I just bought her a soda ... and I need a ride."

"Name's Monica. What's yours, sweet cheeks?" Monica asked with a come-on smile.

Colin thought for a minute, knowing that he didn't want to give her his real name.

"Walt," Colin said, remembering the name of the young woman's male friend.

"Well, Walt, for another twenty I'll give you a ride. For more money, I'll even take you to Boston." Monica looked Colin up and down.

Colin didn't feel the least bit attracted to Monica.

Maybe the fact that she was willing to go with him took the fun out of it. He wasn't sure but he did need transportation and Monica was willing to provide it. He accepted her offer.

Flight 228 touched down in Dallas. Connor and Kate walked to their next gate, dodging the hordes of people and roller bags. Once at their gate, Kate went to find something to eat while Connor turned on his cell phone to check his messages. Connor saw that he had one voice mail. Playing the message, he learned that it was from Colin's father, Edward Bolton. Connor looked at his watch and his next boarding pass. He figured they had about an hour to wait, so he dialed Bolton's number. He waited for the housekeeper to get Bolton on the line. Connor wondered if Colin had called or gone back to his dad's house.

"This is Edward."

"Mr. Bolton, I got your message asking me to call you. First, let me tell you that we're in the Dallas airport waiting for our next flight. The noise is bad here but what can I do for you?"

"Detective…"

Silence followed. Connor thought his phone had dropped the call.

"Mr. Bolton, are you still there?"

"Yes. I'm sorry. What I'm about to tell you is very hard for me to say … Colin has been in trouble before, Detective."

"Mr. Bolton, we figured as much. Could you tell us what kind of trouble and why there aren't any records?"

Connor again waited for Edward to speak. More silence followed and Connor knew that Bolton was struggling with what to say.

"It started at a young age, things like peeking at girls in the bathroom…"

"That would explain why it didn't show up on his records."

"No, no, that's not all and it's not the reason why things aren't showing up. Detective, it was me."

"You?"

"It was me. I had my attorney make sure that those things would never be found."

"Okay, was there more than the issue of the girls' bathroom?"

"Yes, he was accused of rape twice. Once it was an elderly woman and another time a child." As the last words left his mouth, Edward felt relief. He had carried Colin's secret and been co-dependent for all these years.

Connor sat, digesting this new information. Kate returned and sat next to him. By the look on his face, she knew that something was up.

"Mr. Bolton, can you tell me, were these two females found dead or alive?"

Kate now knew who Connor was talking to. He tilted his head toward hers and lifted the phone from his ear so that she could also listen.

"Both were alive."

"You said your attorney had things covered up, but Colin should have had to register as a sex offender at the very least."

"Detective Maxwell, that was my fault. I didn't want this to follow my son for the rest of his life. My attorney had Colin admitted to a mental hospital each time. Colin went but was released after six months both times."

"Six months for rape!" Connor said, a little too loudly, causing a woman sitting across from him to get up and walk to another seat.

"Yes. After the second time, my attorney told me that I had to show tough love and stop bailing out Colin when he got in trouble. I didn't listen to him and I should have. I can assure you, this time Colin is on his own."

"I know I asked this before, but I'll ask again. Do you have any knowledge of where he is? Has he called you?"

"No. I promise that I'll call you and the Boston police if I hear from him or if he shows up here."

Kate heard their flight being called and motioned to Connor.

"Mr. Bolton, our flight is being called. Would you text me the attorney's name and contact information so that I have it when I get back to Lakewood?"

CHAPTER 31

Monica took I-40, following the white line ribbon of highway from Tulsa, Oklahoma east. She glanced over at the man whom she'd met in the mall barely an hour ago. Was his name really Walt? Or John or Henry? It didn't matter. She wanted out of Tulsa and he said he'd pay the way. He was asleep, snoring like her Uncle Raymond's old bloodhound, Marvin Gaye. The man had said that he didn't want to listen to the radio, that music bothered him. So, she drove in silence except for the hum of her tires caressing the payment.

She knew that he had a wad of cash in his wallet. It had been hard to miss when he'd paid for the gas in her car. A thought lurked in the shadows of her mind that he could be a bank robber. Monica glanced at him again. He was well dressed, had a nice smile, and was well-groomed. She shook her head as if to get that idea out of her brain. He was a nice man whose car had broken down in Tulsa and he had to get back to Boston. He'd said that his father would send for his car or that he'd go back for it.

Monica wondered what Mister Walt's car was. Probably one of those fancy BMWs, Caddies, or Mercedes. Whatever it was, she'd bet it had one of those GPS things that told you how to get to where you wanted to go and blue … blue fang or something. She couldn't remember what it was called, but it let you talk on your cell phone with the speakers in your car.

Colin's face was turned toward the window. Monica returned her attention to the road and the mile markers. She wondered where he'd want to stop for the night. She hoped it would be one of those classy hotels she had seen only on TV or in magazines.

Out of her peripheral vision, she saw a motorist passing her on the passenger side. Monica had been so deep in thought that she had forgotten to move back to the right lane after passing that stinky cattle truck.

She glanced over to see the driver looking at her car. He passed her, then slowed down until their cars were side by side.

Jake Mercer had just finished his business meeting, packed his suitcase, and gotten started on the road. When he had passed the lady on I-40, about forty miles outside Tulsa, he had slowed his car. He wanted to take another look at the passenger in the vehicle he had just passed. When he was even with the car, he studied the man's face. It was him! Jake was sure of it. He had watched the news while having breakfast at the hotel earlier that morning. The man was a wanted criminal. It was him, he said to himself. He slowed down and tried to get the female driver's attention. Did she know who he was —or was she his next victim?

Jake didn't want to honk his horn, which would have awakened the man. Instead, he pulled up next to the woman, as close as he could, and motioned for her to pull over.

Monica refused to look in his direction. She swerved toward the opposite side of the lane to get away from him. "What the hell is this guy doing?" she muttered.

Jake pulled up alongside her once more. This time, the woman raised her middle finger and sped up. Jake picked up his cell phone and dialed 911. Nothing happened. He peered at the phone in his hand. No bars. No service.

"Great!" Jake said to himself. While this was a busy stretch of interstate highway, all he could see were miles and miles of pastureland with a smattering of cattle grazing on it. He decided that if she refused to pull over, he would come up behind her and snap a photo of her license plate. Then, as soon as he got into the next town or had service on his phone, he could provide the authorities with that information.

Jake got about a car length behind her, then braced both wrists on the steering wheel with the camera app ready. As he tried to focus his camera on her license plate, she hit her brakes.

"Shit!" yelled Jake as he swerved to avoid hitting the back of her car. He applied the brakes and ended up on the shoulder of the highway, dropping his cell phone to the floor.

"What the hell…?" Colin woke up and looked over at Monica. She was laughing as she watched the car on the shoulder of the road, surrounded by a cloud of dirt. Colin turned around and looked over the seat.

"Some guy was being a jerk. He wanted me to pull over. When I didn't, he came right up on my bumper."

Colin continued looking at the car on the side of the road until the dust settled. No light bar on top or in front. Was he safe? Was this just some nut on the highway?

Monica stopped for gas and they decided to make it to Memphis. The sunlight was giving way to darkening skies as the "Welcome to Memphis" sign greeted them.

"Where do you want to stay for the night?"

Monica asked.

"You pick," Colin said.

"I saw a Hampton Inn sign back there a ways. The exit is about a mile up from here."

"Sure, whatever," Colin said, looking around the town as the car pulled off the exit.

At check-in, Colin requested two rooms and paid cash. When the front desk clerk requested a credit card for any additional services, like movies or room service, Colin said he didn't have one. He didn't want to take the chance of the cops following the paper trail of his credit card, so he had taken out several large cash advances prior to this. The desk clerk agreed that he could leave a refundable two-hundred-dollar deposit for each room. Colin pulled out the cash, then told Monica to order room service for dinner and put it on his tab.

Once inside her room, Monica fell over on the bed. A girl could get used to this, she thought to herself. She had to call her friend, Jessica, back in Tulsa and tell her about her great adventure.

Colin tossed his duffle bag into his room and then left the hotel in search of an auto parts store for a wrench. He had seen one about a block from the hotel. He returned to his room at around two o'clock in the morning and ordered room service. As he ate, he looked out over the parking lot. He could see Monica's red Toyota. About four parking spots over was another Toyota Corolla that looked similar to hers. If a cop ran the plate, he could assume that they'd had the car repainted. This was just insurance, Colin reasoned with himself.

He left the room with the wrench in his pocket. First, he removed Monica's plate, then walked around the parking lot. When he was confident that no one was around, he quickly swapped plates with the other Toyota.

CHAPTER 32

Jake Mercer sat at the state police headquarters in Nashville, Tennessee. Nervously, he tapped his fingers on the metal desktop while he waited for a detective to be called in from the field. Jake had already called his boss and explained why he'd be late for the next meeting. The second call was to his wife in Kansas City, Missouri to tell her about the woman in the red Toyota, driving with a wanted man on I-40. He was about to tell her how he'd been run off the road when the door opened.

A six-foot-something man who looked like he bench-pressed cars in his spare time entered the room and took a seat. Jake disconnected his call and put away his phone.

"Mr. Mercer, I'm State Police Detective Wes Wyatt. I called the Lakewood Police Department. It would appear the passenger you saw in the red Toyota does match the description of Colin Bolton, the man they're looking for. However, the female driver doesn't match the missing woman. Would you mind repeating for me what happened?"

"Jake, please call me Jake. I had seen the news in the hotel I stayed at in Tulsa and…"

Detective Wyatt interrupted Jake. "What hotel would that be?"

"I stayed at the Best Western. Does that matter?"

"Mr. Mercer, I just need to get all the background. When you left the…" Wes looked at his notepad and rubbed the stubble on his chin. "Where did you go?"

"Well, I packed, then gassed up my car."

"Did you notice the red Toyota and its occupants at the gas station?"

"No. Well, if they did go to the same gas station, I don't remember seeing them."

"When did you first notice the red Toyota?"

"Outside of Tulsa. I passed several other cars. Once I got beyond the city limits, there were a few other cars. The lady driving the red Toyota was in the passing lane but wasn't doing the speed limit. I passed in the right-hand lane. That's when I noticed him, the guy from the news. He was sleeping with his head facing my direction." Jake waited as the detective wrote down things in his notebook.

"The woman you described to the officer on duty

doesn't match the woman whom the Lakewood PD is looking for. Are you sure of her age?"

"I can't be positive on the age, Detective. But she looked to me to be around early to mid-thirties."

With that, the detective pulled his cell phone from his pocket, scrolled through a few messages, and then stopped. He set his phone on the interview table and slid it across to Jake.

"Could this be the woman?" Detective Wyatt asked.

Jake leaned over and took a closer look at the photo of a young woman. Then he looked up at the detective.

"No, this woman is too young. The woman driving was much older. She had a hard look.

"A hard look?" Detective Wyatt asked.

"You know, like a lady who hangs out in bars."

"You're sure? Take another look."

Jake did as the detective instructed.

"This woman," Jake pointed to the photo on the phone's display. "This woman is much younger. Her hairstyle is different and it's the wrong color."

"I'll be right back," Detective Wyatt said. He excused himself and left the room.

Once in the hallway, he dialed Detective Bob Barton, whom he had spoken to earlier. Bob had sent Lacey's photo to him in the off chance that she was still with Colin and alive. Detective Wyatt left a voice mail for Detective Barton, stating that he had shown the photo of the victim to the witness and that he had said that she was not the woman in the red Toyota. He further told him that he would send the witness's contact information to him.

Detective Wyatt re-entered the room and took a seat.

"Is there anything else? A bumper sticker, a dent on the car, or any part of the license plate you remember?"

"I have this." Jake pulled out his cell phone and handed it to the detective.

The detective looked at a blurry shot of the back of the red Toyota. The image was above the license plate.

"I'm sorry. When I tried to take the photo, that's when she slammed on the brakes. I dropped my phone and ran off the side of the road to avoid hitting her car. Honestly, I didn't think I had even managed to get this photo."

"Mr. Mercer, I'd like to give your phone to our tech guy here. He may be able to do something with this photo to clear it up. It should take only a few minutes. They'll get the photo off your phone and get your phone back to you so that you can be on your way. Also, I've given your contact information to the Lakewood police in case they need to talk to you."

The next morning, Monica met Colin for breakfast. Afterward, they loaded their luggage and found a gas station just off the highway. Colin glanced down at the newly acquired license plate he had put on Monica's car the night before. He watched to see if she noticed that her plate had been swapped with another. Colin reasoned that most people had no clue what alphanumeric combination was on their license plate. After they topped off the tank, Colin gave Monica cash to get them some snacks and drinks for the road. He told her that he'd wait in the car for her.

As he watched her enter the station, Colin saw a sheriff's department car pull in. Quickly, he bent down to the floorboards, out of the deputy's sight. Monica returned with a bag full of snacks and soda pop as the deputy glanced over at the red Toyota. She proceeded to take everything out of the bag, one item at a time, to show Colin what she had purchased.

Meanwhile, the deputy typed in the license plate and waited to see if the red Toyota was the one that a BOLO had been issued for. As he waited, he watched the car.

"Let get a move on!" Colin snapped.

Monica jumped and quickly stuffed everything back into the bag. She pushed a lock of hair behind her ear and pulled away from the pump.

CHAPTER 33

Flight 2220 touched down on the Lakewood runway. As the large aircraft slowly rolled toward gate B2, Kate looked around the cabin. Passengers were gathering their belongings like tired children forced to pick up their toys. Chatter rose as people conversed with one another. Connor reached inside his sports coat pocket, retrieved his cell phone, and switched out of airplane mode. As soon as the bars lit up, indicating the signal strength, he heard a series of chimes announcing that he had text messages.

Kate looked over at Connor. "Anything important?"

"Looks like two messages from Bob Barton," Connor said, trying to read the message while the plane taxied to the gate.

"Sundae okay?"

"No. I mean it's not about Sundae. He says he got a call from out of state that Colin was spotted on I-40 just outside of Tulsa. Seems he was a passenger in a red Toyota with a lady driving."

"Was it Lacey?

Connor continued to read. "He said the state police detective in Nashville showed Lacey's photo to the witness, who was certain the woman wasn't Lacey."

"Nashville? I thought you said he was spotted in Tulsa."

"The witness drove to Nashville, Tennessee and stopped at the state police headquarters. He told them that he had seen a photo of Colin on the news and that the man in the Toyota had looked like Colin."

"Did he get a plate number?"

"No. The woman ran the witness off the highway when he got close to her car. They have a photo that the witness attempted to take of the car. Their IT lab is working to enhance the photo but the detective told Bob that the image didn't capture the plate at all. Looks like the second message is the witness's contact information.

"He must be heading back to his father's house," Kate said.

Connor didn't reply. He was already typing a text to Bob, requesting that he call Boston PD and ask them to place someone at Colin's father's house.

Connor thought that if Colin had left Lakewood on the run, heading east, there was a good chance that he was heading back to his father.

If Colin felt that his father disapproved of what he had done to Lacey and the cab driver, the chance was good that his father could become another one of Colin's victims. Connor hit "send" on his message, then slid his phone back into his pocket.

Passengers had already stood up and were going through the overheads like shoppers at a Black Friday sale, grabbing their carry-on luggage even though they had to wait in the aisle to disembark the plane. Connor stretched out his arms in front of him, still seated, waiting to stand up and exit. Kate ran her fingers through her hair in an attempt to undo what she had done while she took a cat nap on the flight from Dallas to Lakewood.

Monica looked at the gas gauge, which read a quarter of a tank. She started exiting the freeway for a large gas station that catered to both truckers and motorists. Colin woke up to see the truck stop coming into sight.

"No, not there! Head up the road and look for a smaller gas station," he said.

Monica veered off the exit lane and emerged back on the freeway.

"No radio while we drive, now no large gas stations? Is there something I should know about you?"

Monica was joking, but her comment upset Colin. "Look, I'm paying you to take me. I'm not paying you for the third degree."

After that, Monica worried that she'd hurt his feelings. More so, she was beginning to feel that something was off with him. She couldn't quite put her finger on it. He didn't like to eat inside at a diner or a fast food place. He always made her go in to get the food and then bring it out for them. Or could the endless, mindless, brain-numbing miles she drove in total silence while he slept be playing tricks on her mind? Regardless, if she had the opportunity, she decided to take a photo of him when he wasn't looking, then send it to her friend back in Tulsa.

However, right now she needed gas and to ask how to get back to I-70. She had never been good with directions or, for that matter, been on a road trip this long. With him sleeping most the time, Monica had managed to end up someplace in Kentucky. She had to head north, toward the top of the United States. She hoped that the man she knew as Walter wouldn't get mad at her, but he also appeared to have no idea where they were.

Monica spotted a sign up ahead for a Shell station. "Would this station be okay? I really need to pee," she said.

Colin could see the station coming into sight. "That will work."

Like before, he pumped the gas while Monica paid and used the restroom. As Monica left the restroom, she noticed some snacks and grabbed a bag of popcorn, as well as a soda for herself and one for Colin. As she stood in line to pay for the snacks, she looked up at the flat-screen TV hanging on the wall behind the cash registers. Monica wished the damn thing were on. For miles, she'd heard only road noise and Colin's snoring—no radio or TV. By the time they stopped for the night, it was late and she was too tired to do anything but sleep.

As she left the station, Monica grabbed her cell phone and quickly took a photo of Colin as he was checking a rear tire. Then she slipped her phone back into her purse. That evening, once she had checked into her room, Monica sent the photo to her best friend. Just in case. After that, she crawled into bed and fell asleep. The following morning, she and Colin loaded up and headed out.

Back in Tulsa, Monica's friend, Jessica, woke up. She grabbed her cell phone and a cup of coffee. Sitting cross-legged on her bed, Jessica lit up a cigarette. Blue haze from the smoke encircled her as she scrolled through her messages. She stopped when she saw a message from Monica with a photo of her traveling partner. Jessica scrolled by and then scrolled back to the photo and focused on the man's face. She dropped her phone onto the bed.

"Oh, my God, that's him! The man the police are looking for on the news."

She grabbed her phone and hit the speed dial for Monica.

"Oh, oh … she's driving with a mad man!" Jessica said, tapping her long red fingernails on the bedside table. She lit another cigarette even though one was still in her mouth. "Oh, crap!" she blurted once she realized she was already smoking one. Jessica set the newly lit cigarette in the ashtray and nervously puffed on the one in her mouth.

"Pick up your phone!" she said to herself.

What should she do? If she left a message and he checked Monica's phone, that wouldn't be good. She could text but, again, if the man looked at the text, he would read her warning to Monica. Jessica looked at her cat, sitting on the bed and staring at her.

"What do we do? He may already have killed her," she said to the cat. Jessica ended the call to Monica and dialed 911.

The dispatcher spoke in a calm, professional manner. "911, what is your emergency?"

"It's my friend, she's driving with a man … that the police want for abducting a young woman … somewhere."

"Slow down. Where is your friend now?" asked the dispatcher.

"Slow down? My friend is out there on the highway, God knows where, with some crazed killer."

"Ma'am, do you know the man's name?"

"That guy. The guy they had on the news. He abducted some young woman. They had his picture on the news last night."

CHAPTER 34

Jessie, frustrated with the 911 operator, hung up on her. She quickly threw on some clothes and then drove to the police station. Swinging the door open, she entered. Her thick-soled sandals made a slapping sound each time her heel hit the floor. The desk sergeant in charge looked up as he heard the noise. His mouth fell open as he watched the woman coming toward him. She was wearing a kaleidoscope of colors: bright orange capri pants, a purple V-neck tee shirt, and electric-blue-framed glasses. He couldn't tell if her lipstick was black or deep purple. Several beaded bracelets and necklaces—all in various colors and none matching any of the clothes she was wearing—accessorized the outfit. The sergeant was certain this woman hadn't come off the latest clothing designer's runway. Or at least, he hoped she hadn't.

"How can I help?" asked the sergeant, thinking to himself that maybe she needed someone to dress her in the morning.

"It's my friend Monica. See, she met this dude at the mall the other day," Jessie said. She lifted her large squish-worm-green handbag, which landed with a thud on the desk.

The sergeant moved his right hand to the butt of his gun, just in case the thud was a gun.

Jessie rooted through her bag and began placing things on the counter in front of the sergeant. He watched as she laid out a package of tissues, two lipsticks, a pack of gum, a mirror, a pen, what looked to be an address book, and an unused tampon.

"Here it is!" she exclaimed as she pulled out her cellphone.

The cell phone case was decorated with all colors of bling. As he let out a heavy sigh, the sergeant thought to himself that this woman was a total piece of work and wondered what planet she came from. He watched as she scrolled through some messages and then stopped.

"This all could have been handled when I called 911 this morning but the woman just didn't understand me!"

The sergeant thought to himself, 'Gee, I wonder why.'

Jesse thrust her cell phone toward the sergeant. "See!"

The sergeant carefully looked at the photo. Quickly, he turned around and pulled a large clipboard with two metal rings off the wall. He thumbed through the photos and typed descriptions.

"Finally, a knight in shining armor! Please don't be a loser in aluminum foil," Jess said as she exhaled.

Before the sergeant was able to turn around, Jessie leaned over the counter, exposing her cleavage as she examined the sergeant's butt and smiled.

The sergeant stopped on a page about halfway through his clipboard and turned around. He couldn't help noticing her hanging over the desk and his eyes stopped on her cleavage. Jessie leaned back with a big smile on her face.

"Where and how did you get this photo?" he asked.

"As I was saying, my friend Monica ... She's sort of a loose cannon sometimes ... I just got to keep her on a tight leash, if you know what I mean." She tapped her long fingernails on the glass of her cell phone, pointing at Colin's photo. "At the mall, she met him at the mall, can you imagine? He said he needed a ride and Monica said she would drive him if he'd pay for all the expenses. I saw his photo on the news last night ... He's wanted, right? I know he is. She met this dude and, poof, she was gone like the wind!"

Jessie looked at the sergeant's name on his

uniform while he compared the photo on a BOLO printout to the one on Jessie's phone.

"Do you have any idea where this was taken?"

Jess turned the phone around and scrolled up to the text in the message. She pointed. The text read, "somewhere in Kentucky and I'm a little lost and need to head upward to I-70."

"Let me call in our detective to talk with you. You can have a seat over there." The sergeant pointed to the chairs across from his desk.

"Oh, by the way, is there a Mrs. Blankenship?" Jess asked the sergeant.

He looked at her, confused.

"I saw your name tag and was just wondering if there was a missus?"

By the time Connor and Kate grabbed their baggage and headed to the police department, Bob and Sundae were waiting for them with a sheet of paper at the dispatch area.

"Got something for you." Bob handed the paper to Connor. "Let's go back to our desks."

Connor read as they all walked down the hall.

"So, this woman is really with him. Do we know if she went of her own free will or has she been abducted, too?" Connor asked. Finishing the printout, he passed it to Kate.

"From what the Tulsa PD says, last night she sent a text with a photo that matches Colin to her best friend. This morning, the friend woke up, saw the text and photo, and panicked because she thought he matched the photo she'd seen on the local news. In the text, the friend mentioned she thought she was lost and needed to head up to I-70. She also said she was in Kentucky someplace.

"The desk sergeant said that, by the looks of the photo, they were gassing up the car. Sandy has already pulled all the info on the person with him. Her name is Monica Braxton. We know they're in a red Toyota and now we have a license plate number. Sandy has already sent out a new BOLO. She has called Colin's father and given him an update, as well as Boston PD. I think he's trying to get back to his daddy."

"I don't think he'll receive a warm welcome if he shows up there," Kate said.

"Oh, this Monica told her friend that the man she's traveling with says his name is Walter. She also said he refuses to go into diners. Makes her go in and bring out food. He wants to stop only at small gas stations and gives her cash to go in for anything they need. Refuses to allow her to listen to the radio while she's driving. In short, he's trying his best to stay out of sight and keep her away from any news. What no one really knows is how much this Monica knows. Does she understand she could be his next victim?"

Bob continued. "From what the detective told me in Tulsa, her friend has tried to reach her by phone and can't. The Tulsa PD asked her friend to keep trying to reach her, but to not leave voicemail or text on her cell phone in case he sees it. They got the number and gave it to us as well. They've tried blocking their incoming number from her caller ID but still no luck."

"That can't be good," Kate said.

CHAPTER 35

At the last gas station, Monica found out she didn't need to get on I-70. That wouldn't have been a problem, but the night before, she'd told her best friend, Jessie, that she was heading north to I-70 from Kentucky. Now she worried that if Jessie did send someone to look for her, they would be looking in the wrong place. Monica was becoming increasingly nervous about Walter's behavior. After the last fill-up, the station owner, a nice man, drew her a map.

Once in the car, Walter insisted on examining the piece of paper. The farther east they drove, the more paranoid he got. Maybe she should try to leave after dark. After all, they had separate rooms. How would he even know? Monica tried to hatch a plan as she drove. Once they were supposed to be asleep in their rooms, she would grab her things and quietly exit.

He could find another person to take him to Boston. But how would she do it? She didn't have enough money to get back home to Tulsa.

She'd been stashing away a few dollars in change from the cash he gave her when she purchased gas, food, or snacks. He never checked the receipts or seemed to care, which she thought was odd. Tonight, she needed to see if she had enough money to get home, even if it meant sleeping in her car or not eating along the way. Also, maybe Jessie had found out something about Walter.

Monica pointed her red Toyota toward I-64 East. Then, doing her best to follow the hand-drawn map, she merged onto what seemed to be an endless series of roads: I-77, I-68, I-81, and some others she'd already forgotten. As they neared the exit for I-78 into Allentown, she'd been behind the wheel a little over fourteen hours. She asked Walter if they could spend the night in Allentown. Once he agreed, he found a small roadside motel just outside the city limits that suited him. They pulled in and Monica went in with cash to get two rooms. After she paid, she went outside and told Walter the man was demanding more for the damage deposit, which was a hundred and fifty dollars per room, since she had paid with cash and not credit. At this point, she knew full well that Walter would never go inside to argue the point with the desk clerk. Walter dug out the cash and gave it to her.

The rooms were paid for, so when she returned to the lobby, she simply asked where the rooms were and pocketed the three hundred dollars that Colin had given to her. That was her "go home money," she thought to herself.

They checked into their rooms and she ordered two pizzas to be delivered to her room. She would pay and take his pizza to his room, then go back and eat hers. She vowed to not allow herself to fall asleep, not tonight. Tonight, she was heading back to Tulsa. As soon as she got back to her room, she tucked the three hundred away in a safe place.

She had talked Walter into gassing up before they'd stopped for the night, so the Toyota was sitting on a full tank, ready for her to go. Walter hadn't slept as much today while she drove, so she figured he'd get a good night's rest and he wouldn't discover until morning that she had left.

After she ate, Monica pulled out her cell phone and noticed she had no service. Still, she typed out a text message to Jessie, explaining her plan and telling her that she was leaving tonight without him. Monica figured that once she was in an area with cell service, the message would hopefully go through. Their first day on the road, Walter had told her that her phone was to remain off. Tonight would be different. As she backtracked her way home, she could listen to her radio and leave her phone on.

It was a little after midnight when Monica

bolted up in bed. She had just laid her head on the pillows for a few minutes but had been out like a light. She grabbed her things, ran a brush through her hair, took her phone off the charger, and looked out the motel window. Nothing was out there but the stillness of the night. The door creaked as she opened it. She stopped, put her bag out first, and then turned sideways so she didn't have to open the door farther and risk making more noise. She looked both ways. The window in Colin's room was dark. She assumed he must be asleep by now.

Slowly, she walked out to the car. However, she had forgotten that the night before, she had used the key bob to set the Toyota's alarm system. Therefore, once she clicked it to unlock it, it would chirp.

"Shit!" she said out loud, thinking she should have locked it with the key and not set the alarm.

Monica stood next to the driver's side door. Slowly, she placed her hand on the handle. She held her small suitcase with the other. She closed her eyes as an early morning breeze washed over her and then she took a deep breath. Her heart was pounding so loudly, she was sure Colin could hear it. She transferred her bag to the last few fingers on her right hand and held the key bob between the index finger and thumb on the same hand. She planned to toss the bag on the passenger seat, get herself in, insert the key in the ignition, back out of the parking lot, and drive away from the motel as fast as she could.

She thought she heard something behind her. Oh, God. Her breath caught in her throat. Turning slowly, she saw a stray dog wandering through the parking lot. Monica let out a sigh of relief.

Looking back at Walter's window, she saw that it was still dark. It was time for her to make her move. One ... two ... three. She depressed the key bob and jumped into the car. As she got in, Monica's hands were shaking so badly that she dropped her keys on the floor. Quickly, she locked her doors. With only the light from the parking lot, she felt around until she found her keys. Lifting them, she stabbed the keys three times before she got them into the ignition. The Toyota engine turned over and she threw the car into reverse. Monica backed out without headlights, not turning them on until she was back out on the street in front of the motel. She had been holding her breath and now breathed a sigh of relief.

As she drove, Monica reached over for her purse. She fished around until she pulled out her cell phone. She had bars now and knew Jessie had received her message. Or had she? The digital clock on the dash read 1:20 am. With her headlights now on, Monica looked around. No one was out. The street was empty except for her car. She saw the green exit sign to I-78 West and signaled to get onto the ramp. As her car made a slight turn, she thought she heard something behind her. 'It's probably my suitcase,' she thought. Then she looked over to the passenger seat and remembered that her suitcase was sitting right there beside her, not in the back seat. 'It's just my imagination playing tricks on me,' she thought to herself. Monica listened carefully but did not hear any sound other than the road noise of her tires on the payment.

It was now around two o'clock in the morning. Her cell phone rang and she jumped. Who would be calling her at this hour? She ran through everything she and Walter had talked about. She knew she hadn't given him her cell phone number, so who was calling at this hour?

"Hello."

"Monica Braxton, this is the Lakewood Police Department. Are you alone at this time?" the Lakewood dispatcher asked.

"Lakewood Police? I think you have the wrong number," Monica said. She started to disconnect the call.

"Monica!" the dispatcher yelled, "Don't hang up the phone! Is the man you're traveling with within earshot of this call?"

"No, not at all. He was acting so weird … I left Allentown, Pennsylvania at around one o'clock this morning without him. Why?"

"Listen to me. Monica, you need to give me your

nearest mile marker. Don't stop or go back for him. He is extremely dangerous. Do you hear me?"

"Yes, but you're scaring me."

"Just keep driving and give me your location I'll have a Pennsylvania State Police officer intercept you. He will protect you. Can you please tell me where Colin is?"

"Who the hell is Colin? Is this some sort of prank?"

"Monica, this is no prank. Your friend, Jessie, came into the Tulsa Police Department with the photo you sent last night. The man you've been traveling with is wanted and is extremely dangerous. Do not go back to him, do you understand? What highway are you on?"

"I-7. I don't know what mile marker I'm at, but you are r-e-a-l-l-y scaring me."

Monica thought she saw a movement behind her car. She looked up into the rearview mirror. As she took her eye off the highway and stared into the rearview mirror, her car skidded onto the shoulder of the road. Her front tires hit the road braille, making a bumping sound. She quickly pulled the car back into the driving lane. The thing was not behind the car, it was in the backseat. She looked around and saw Colin sitting there. As she did, he grabbed the phone out of her hand.

She screamed, "He's in my backseat!"

A struggle could be heard and the call was disconnected.

"Monica, Monica!" The dispatcher yelled into the phone but the line was dead. She called Monica's number again but the call went straight to voicemail.

CHAPTER 36

The ring from Connor's cellphone on the bedside table woke him up. At first, he was disoriented, having just flown in from Boston's Logan Airport that day. In the darkness of his bedroom, his phone started to slip from his hand but he was able to catch it before it hit the floor.

"Hello," he said, trying his best to clear his throat and sound awake.

"Detective, I'm really sorry to wake you but we have a situation," the Lakewood dispatcher said.

"And what would that situation be?"

"Detective, you had left word with Sandy late this evening for the dispatch team to keep calling this person, Monica Braxton. I called several times and got no answer until around two o'clock Eastern time. I did as you instructed, which was to first ask if Colin was within earshot. She said no. She stated she had just snuck out of the motel room and was driving back home alone."

"Great, what motel? What city did she leave Colin at?"

"Ah … Not great, sir. I was attempting to ascertain her location. She said she had been on the road from about one or one-thirty in the morning. She left a city called Allentown, Pennsylvania. I asked what highway and mile marker she was at and said that I was going to call the Pennsylvania State Police to escort her to their headquarters for protection and questioning."

Connor interrupted her. "Did you get the motel Colin was at?"

"See … that's the thing, sir. She told me she was on I-78."

"Mile marker and what motel?" Connor demanded.

"Sir, I heard her scream, a very, very scared scream. Then it sounded like two people fighting. I could hear a male's voice and hers. Then the line went dead."

Connor was sitting on the edge of his bed by now. "Call the Pennsylvania State Police. Request that they look for a red Toyota with the license plate number we have for Monica Braxton. Request that they go both east and west. We have to remember that she's not from that area. It's nighttime and she's scared. She could have taken off in any direction.

Next, call Sandy and request that she come in to the PD and help us. Ask her to get in touch with her friend at the phone company and have them ping Monica's phone for a location. Next, I want you and her to start calling hotels and motels to see if anyone who matches Monica's description checked in there this evening.

"Also, we need Pennsylvania's county and city PDs notified. I'll come in. It will take me about fifteen minutes."

"Sir, I hope Monica is okay. I really did ask her if she was alone."

"I understand. Get started and I'll be there in a few."

Monica gripped the steering wheel hard. She was sure if she could see them, her knuckles would be white as the sheets on her bed at home. Colin had taken off his belt and wrapped it around her neck as he sat behind her in the backseat.

"I wondered how long it would take you to figure out who I was," Colin said sarcastically.

"Listen, Walter … ah, Colin, whoever you are. I don't know what you did and I don't want to. Just let me go. You can have my car and go to Boston or wherever you wish. Just please let me go," Monica sobbed.

"Turn the car around. You're not heading in the correct direction. Don't put the flashers on. Just drive the car like nothing is wrong. No turn signals on unless you're changing lanes or turning."

"If the police know my name, then surely they have my license plate number. Did you ever think of that?"

"That's where you're wrong. The first night we were on the road, I switched your license plate with one from another car. So, they may know you're in a red Toyota ... hmm, I wonder how many red Toyota Corollas are out there on the road. Would you like to venture a guess? Do you honestly think they'll pull over all of them? With the wrong plate and tag? I don't think so. Now turn the damn car around at the next area that crosses the road and head back east. And let go of your cell phone."

Colin chuckled and jerked the belt around her neck with his free hand to show her that he meant business. Monica reluctantly handed him her cell phone.

"There," he said, pointing to an area to cross back to the other side of the highway. He rolled down the rear window "Now wait here."

Monica wondered if her life would end there on I-78. Would they ever find her?

Colin looped the belt through the buckle around her neck and got out, holding it in one hand. She wondered if she stepped on the gas would she be free of him or would it break her neck? An open-bed truck drove by and Colin heaved the cell phone into the truck's bed. Climbing back into the backseat, he told her to head for Boston. Monica did as instructed and pulled back onto I-78 in the opposite direction.

When Connor arrived at the police department, the dispatchers, Sandy, and Kate were already on the phones, calling motels and hotels in the area, with no luck. The Pennsylvania State Police were looking both ways on I-78. The ping from Monica's cell phone indicated she was moving in a westward direction. The Pennsylvania State Police were following the location as it had stopped.

Heading east on I-78, Pennsylvania State Police patrolman James Rand spotted a red Toyota. He cautiously pulled closer and ran the license plate, then backed off, waiting to see what came back. His computer listed the plate as belonging to a green Toyota Corolla. With the plate number, and the issuing state not matching, he had a gut feeling that something wasn't right. With not much else going on at this early hour of the morning, he decided to stay behind the car and observe it. It appeared to have only one passenger: a female driver.

A few miles later, he thought he noticed a head pop up in the backseat but only for a minute. He thought it may have been a child. Or maybe not. He engaged his lights and pulled closer. Monica saw the lights of the patrol car at the same time Colin did.

"Keep driving!" Colin ordered.

"But it's a police officer. I promise, I'm doing the speed limit." She choked out the last words as Colin pulled harder on the belt.

"Pull the car over!" the patrolman ordered over his car's PA system.

Monica started to pull the car over to the shoulder of the road.

"I told you to keep going," Colin yelled in her ear.

Patrolman Rand watched the car swerve several times. He trained his spotlight into the back window and could clearly see an adult in the backseat. He called in his location to request backup, then continued following the red Toyota.

Suddenly, the Toyota pulled onto the shoulder. The back door burst open and a man ran from the car. Patrolman Rand quickly gave his location and told his dispatcher he was after a male on foot.

Colin ran as fast as he could to the tree line. If he could get into the forest, he knew he had a chance of hiding. Once the cop was gone, he could hitch a ride. Monica sat in her car, choking, pulling at the narrow belt, but it was embedded in her skin. Finally, she pulled the belt loose from her neck. She looked around to see the cop and Colin disappear into the trees.

Patrolmen Rand heard something to his left. He stopped dead in his tracks and just listened. Again, he heard it. He reasoned with himself that at this hour, it could be a deer or any number of critters that roamed the forests at night. He walked slowly in the direction of the noise. He came to a dry ditch and turned on his flashlight. There he saw a man lying prone in the ditch. He unholstered his weapon.

"Get up, hands on your head," Rand commanded.

Colin got up, turned, and ran off. Rand holstered his weapon and took off after Colin. Once close enough, Patrolman Rand jumped and managed to tackle Colin. As the two rolled in the pine needles and dried leaves on the forest floor, Colin struggled for the patrolman's sidearm. When James pushed Colin to one side, Colin launched back at the patrolman. Pinning him down, he reached for a fist-sized rock, which he smashed into the officer's forehead. Rand struggled to remain conscious as the trees overhead began to spin and darkness enveloped him. Colin pulled the officer's service weapon and flashlight, then fled. In the distance, he could hear sirens. He knew he had to hide and get as far as he could from the area.

Monica looked up as a second patrol car and then a third screeched to a stop.

"The man and the police officer ran off into the trees." Monica choked out the words and pointed.

"Call an ambulance for her," one state police officer said to the other, then took off on foot in the direction in which Monica had pointed.

CHAPTER 37

Connor called the Pennsylvania State Police and asked if I-78 was, by any chance, a toll road. The dispatcher said it was. He asked if the toll area had any cameras and, if so, how he could obtain video footage from the day before. The dispatcher put Connor on hold. After several minutes, she came back on the line.

"Detective Maxwell, thank you for your patience. I was able to find out that the I-78 toll area does have video cameras ... but the system was down for repair yesterday afternoon. It was well into the night before they had it up and running."

"Damn!" Connor said.

"Detective, I was just notified by another dispatcher that they located a red Toyota. The woman is okay and is being taken to the hospital for neck injuries. However, so is our officer. Colin

Bolton overpowered him when he ran into the forest and now he has the officer's service weapon."

"Son of a…" Connor hit the desk with his fist.

Kate and Sandy turned and listened as Connor put the call on speakerphone.

"Detective, we have several officers out there looking for him."

"My partner and I will catch the first flight out. What airport should we fly into?"

"That would be Lehigh Valley International Airport in Allentown, Pennsylvania."

"My dispatcher will call you back and give you our flight information as soon as we know."

Once Sandy overheard the airport, she quickly returned to her office and booked a flight for Connor and Kate to Lehigh Valley International Airport.

Early the following morning, Connor, Kate, and Sundae touched down. The state police had a patrolman there to pick them up and take them to Monica's car.

Colin, in his haste to elude the patrolman, had left his bag on the floor of Monica's car. When Sandy called to give all the flight details to the Pennsylvania dispatcher, the dispatcher had told Sandy about the bag. Sandy had asked for the car to remain there until Connor and Kate arrived. She sent a text to both Kate and Connor that Colin's bag was in the backseat, waiting for Sundae.

Once Connor and Kate got to the red Toyota that had been left on the shoulder of the highway, Connor put on latex gloves, then opened Colin's bag. He let Sundae into the back seat and allowed her to sniff the bag.

"Find Colin," Connor instructed. Off went Sundae with the white tip of her tail high in the air.

Connor, Kate, and a Pennsylvania state patrolman took off after her. Sundae ran through the trees and bushes, stopped, then turned left. She stopped again, sniffing all around a cluster of trees. She then ran, zig-zagging from left to right, down to a dry ditch bank and scampered up the opposite side to another tight cluster of trees. There, Connor spotted blood on a dead branch and leaves. He deduced that the blood probably belonged to the highway patrolmen whom Colin had overpowered.

From there, Sundae tracked up a hill where the forest thickened. Connor called Sundae back and pulled a portable water bowl from his belt. He let Sundae drink as they all rested. After a few more minutes, Connor gave the command for Sundae to find Colin.

Sundae was off once again, darting through the endless clusters of trees and up a hill. Once they emerged from the trees, Connor could see Sundae heading in the direction of what looked like a farmhouse. Connor called Sundae back.

"Do you know if anyone lives there?" Connor asked the patrolman.

"Not sure, but I think that's Old Man Sutter's place."

"Does your radio work out here?" Connor asked.

The patrolman checked. They could hear the dispatcher answer back.

"Ask them if there's a phone number for Sutter and see if he's home. Tell him to not say anything but see if the man sounds like he's in any distress."

Within a few minutes, the Pennsylvania dispatcher came back on the radio and said that there was no answer on the landline.

"Ask for backup and give them our location. Sundae and I will start over. You and Kate wait until backup gets here," Connor said.

He and Sundae began walking toward the old house. They entered the property from a tree line behind the home. Slowly, they worked their way around, using the house for cover. Connor peered in each window as they made their way around. He couldn't see the upstairs rooms. However, once Connor got to the living room window, he could clearly see that something had happened in the house. Two chairs were overturned, along with a lamp. The glass from the light bulb was scattered across the floor.

Slowly, he stepped onto the porch. Again, using the house as cover, he tried the front door. It was unlocked. Slowly, he turned the doorknob as Sundae waited by his side. Connor motioned his hand for Sundae to get down. The little beagle got down on her belly. Connor listened but didn't hear anything. His gun drawn, he opened the door. Connor checked the living room, kitchen, and bedrooms upstairs. Nothing.

By now, back-up had come in, entering the same way Connor had. They spoke in whispers or simply made hand gestures toward the barn. Connor, Kate, and Sundae moved toward the right side of the barn. Three state police officers moved toward the left.

Once Connor was close to the barn, he heard an engine turn over. A John Deere tractor suddenly burst through the barn door, sending wooden splinters airborne. Colin was behind the wheel.

Connor could see the old farmer bound and bloody, tied up on the barn floor. One of the Pennsylvania State Police officers took aim with a long gun and shot out both of the rear tires. Colin stopped the tractor, jumped off, and took cover behind the large rear wheel of the tractor. Kate untied Mr. Sutter. She told him to stay inside the barn and not to leave until the police said it was safe.

"Colin, this is Detective Maxwell of the Lakewood Police Department. There is no way out of this. Toss out the gun and come out with your hands up," Connor yelled. Then he waited.

When nothing happened, Connor tossed out a large hand tool. Colin fired twice. Connor motioned to Kate with two fingers, meaning he had fired twice. Connor knew that four more shots were left in Colin's revolver unless he had found more ammo in Sutter's house. Connor took a quick step out and Colin fired once more as Connor ducked and rolled back for cover.

"Connor, unless your insurance covers stupidity, you should think twice about that stunt," Kate said.

Connor held up three fingers, meaning the Colin was down to three shots now. He was counting on Colin not knowing or paying attention to how many bullets he had left.

The state police officers were making plans of their own now as they rolled out a bale of straw, followed by two more and then a third. Colin arched around to the other side and fired again.

"And then there were two shots left," Connor whispered to Kate.

Kate watched as another officer heaved a bale farther. Colin didn't fire. Now they all wondered if he had figured out that he had only two shots left. However, by now Connor could hear a chopper off in the distance, nearing their location. He saw the gleaming badge of the Pennsylvania State Police on the side of the helicopter. As it neared, the side door opened. Colin tried to shoot but they were too high for the handgun. Connor held up one finger, meaning that Colin should have only one shot left.

"Colin Bolton, you have no way out. Toss out the gun," said the officer in the chopper, using the PA system.

"Kate, run around behind the barn to the state police officers. Tell them we need to take him alive if we can, to find out what he did with Lacey," Connor said. Kate took off running to let them know.

Several minutes passed. Kate was returning to Connor's side of the barn when Colin burst into a run for the trees. Connor took off at a dead run for him with Sundae right beside him.

"Connor!" Kate yelled.

Connor neared Colin and tackled him. They both rolled in the field as Connor grabbed for the gun. "Drop it, you son of a…!" Connor said.

Colin brought up his hand and pointed the gun at Connor's head.

Connor yelled for Sundae, who sank her teeth into Colin's wrist. Colin managed to get off a shot that just missed Connor's head. Sundae twisted and turned with her teeth still in Colin's wrist.

"You're out of bullets," Connor said.

"Screw you, I don't believe you," Colin said. He pulled the trigger and nothing happened.

Connor kicked Colin off him, knocked the handgun from his clenched fist, tossed him over, and cuffed his hands behind his back. Kate and the other officers ran up to Connor.

Connor, Kate, and Sundae sat waiting for Colin to be led into the interview room. When the door opened, an officer took his cuffs from around Colin's waist belt and attached them to the large metal ring in the table.

"Colin, I'm Detective Maxwell. My partner is Detective Kate Stroup and this is K9 Sundae, whom you met that day in the field."

Colin looked at his left wrist, which had a large bandage around it, then back at Connor. He said nothing, just sat there and stared at them.

"Colin, can you tell us where Lacey Warner is?" Kate asked.

"I want an attorney," Colin said.

CHAPTER 38

The capture of Colin Bolton made the front-page news. It was the top story on every local channel in Lakewood, and it also hit the world news. Nonetheless, there was still no trace of Lacey Warner, the hard-working single mother of three small children—a daughter, a sister, and a friend. No matter what the legal system did to Colin, it could not get him to open up about what happened to her. Was she dead or alive?

Her brother Zackery came by several times a week to see if there were any new developments. Cody Lambert never forgot the woman he had fallen in love with but whom he had never had the chance to tell. Cody learned that the words that were always on the tip of his tongue but that he'd never spoken while with Lacey were the most important words he could have told her. It would haunt him for the rest of his life. Connor was now plagued by not one but two missing women on his watch.

The DA's office had endless meetings with Colin's appointed public defender as well as Colin. Still, there was no Lacey and no body. In a Hail Mary moment, Colin's father Edward flew all the way from Boston and tried his best to get Colin to talk about Lacey. No matter what, Colin refused to budge when it came to information on her whereabouts.

In a last-ditch effort, Connor tried sticking one of his snitches in the cell next to Colin to see if he would talk. And talk he did—about anything and everything except the disappearance of Lacey Warner, the pretty little lady who went to work one night to earn a living and feed her children but never came home. Colin Bolton refused to talk no matter what they tried. It was always the same lather, rinse, and repeat...

While it was extremely hard to try a person for murder without a body, the DA's office set out to do just that. They had forensic evidence that Lacey had been in Colin's trailer house. They had found hair, skin tissue, blood, and a broken fingernail with both her DNA and Colin's. Further, blood had been found in the truck that Colin had taken from Cody Lambert.

Weeks turned into months, and the months managed to slip around the calendar to form a year.

Connor and Sundae never stopped looking. On his days off, Connor and Sundae walked the hills and mountains in and around Lakewood but found nothing.

As another summer gave way to autumn, the leaves changed from green into yellows and reds. One afternoon, two young boys named Jack and Todd decided to get out their four-wheelers for a ride in the sandy hills around Lakewood. They raced up and down, leaving trails of dust in their wake. Todd stopped and waited for Jack to catch up on a high bank over a ravine. As he waited, something caught his eye. It looked odd. The longer he waited for Jack, the more curiosity overwhelmed him. Todd throttled his Honda four-runner down the steep hill. When he was about ten feet away, he turned, creating a cloud of dust, and brought the four-wheeler to an abrupt stop. Once the dust had settled, he stood on the foot rest and looked. 'Is that…?' he thought to himself. No, it couldn't be.

"What the…" Quickly, Todd pulled his cell phone out of his jeans pocket to call Jack. He realized that he had no cell service. Todd looked again. He was sure, so he rode his four-wheeler back up the hill. There, he saw Jack jumping his four-wheeler over a sand hill. He waved but Jack didn't see him. He jumped, then turned the bike and repeated. Todd rode over to the sand hill and hollered. Once Jack saw him, he drove over to see what Todd wanted.

"Dude, come quick..."

"What?"

"Just follow me ... quick!" Todd led the way down the steep ravine to where he had stopped before and then dismounted his bike. Jack followed and they saw what looked to be a woman's body under an apartment-style dryer.

"Dude, that's a dead person! What do we do?"

"We need to call the police."

"Well, call them!" Jack said.

"I can't. I have no bars. Try your phone."

Jack pulled out his phone and dialed 911, but the phone kept breaking up. The dispatcher had no idea what they were calling about.

"We can go back home and call or wherever we get cell service again," Todd said.

"Think we can remember how to get back here?" Jack looked in all directions.

"Ah ... I think so."

Connor, Kate, and Sundae were about to walk out the door when Sandy waved a hand for them to stop. She was talking to a caller on the phone. They waited until she hung up.

"These two boys were out riding their four-wheeler motorbikes. They're sure they found a woman's body out on the westside, in the sandy hills. Do you all want to take the call or should I give it to Bob and Grant? Connor, I think it's her ... I don't know why, I just do," Sandy said.

The boys met with Connor and Kate at their house. From there, they told the detectives that they thought they could find the place again. However, Connor knew his police unit was no match for the rugged terrain in those sand hills. He called in and had the Lakewood Department's four-wheel-drive SUV brought out for them. As they waited for the vehicle, the boys recounted what they had seen.

Once the department SUV had arrived, Connor, Kate, and Sundae loaded into the vehicle and followed the boys on their four-wheelers. The three bounced inside the SUV, the rugged terrain making them feel like three bugs being shaken in a jar.

"I think they're lost," Kate said as she watched the boys try to retrace their paths.

"Do you think we fell for a teenage joke?" Connor asked Kate.

Todd stopped and stood up on the footrest. He looked all around as Connor pulled alongside the four-wheeler.

"I was sure it was here ... somewhere but the sand hills all look the same now," Todd said.

"You sure this is the general area?" Connor asked.

"Well, kinda?"

Connor grabbed the paper bag with Lacey's coat in it. He got out of the SUV and held the coat up to Sundae's nose. "Find Lacey." Connor gave the command and Sundae took off in her zig-zag pattern, her tail held high in the air. She ran around tumbleweeds the size of cars and brush.

"Cool, she can do that?" Jack asked.

"She can," Kate said. They all stood watching Sundae go up and down the sand hills.

"You think the lady was that one in the news last year?" Todd asked.

"We don't know," Kate said.

"What if it isn't that Lacey person? Will she still find the body" Todd asked.

"If there's a body out there, Sundae will find it," Connor said.

The sun had just begun its descent over the mountain to the west. The shadows of the day grew longer and the sky glowed orange with a touch of pink. Sundae was just about out of sight and Connor was about to call off the search until morning when they heard the little dog howl. Connor ran toward her and Kate started after him.

"Detective Stroup," Todd said. "Jump on." He motioned to the back of his four-wheeler.

As they topped the hill to a dry ravine, Kate saw Connor kneeling beside a body. Sundae was at his left side. The two were only silhouettes as the sun gave off the last light of day in the lonely desert. Nonetheless, Kate hoped and prayed that Connor could rest, at least with this case. While it wasn't the outcome anyone wanted, at least the family could find some closure if this was Lacey's body.

Kate walked up to Connor and put her arm on his shoulder. She could see tear stains on the dried bones that lay before him.

"So, is it her, that lady you're looking for?" Todd asked.

"We'll need to run dental records and DNA to be sure," Kate said.

Connor lifted the drier off her head, then kneeled back down with her.

"Let's call it in," Kate said.

"You go up with the boys. She's been out here long enough by herself. I'll stay with her until everyone gets here," Connor said.

Kate looked at Connor, whose back was turned to her. He wiped tears from his eyes.

EPILOGUE

Connor stood on top of the grassy hillside. Below him was a crowd of mourners. He guessed that at least three hundred people sat in metal chairs surrounding a simple casket. Colin's father had offered to pay for all the funeral expenses but Zackary, Lacey's brother, had turned down his offer.

Sofie stood up to sing a solo of *Amazing Grace*. As she did, she looked upward and saw Connor standing on the hillside. He looked so tall up there, taller than the five-foot nine-inch frame she remembered. She knew it was him by the broad shoulders and narrow waist and by the beagle standing at his side. The sun made the badge on his belt gleam. She had known him since high school. He had been a boy then but he was a man now. She had even lived with him for a few years. Sofie had loved him with all her heart. For a birthday present one year, she had given him a nickel-plated handgun—the first handgun he'd ever owned. With that, he became interested in joining the police force. Sofie hadn't minded at first. Then, each time he left for work, she worried. Part of her blamed his choice of employment on that stupid birthday gift she had given him. How could she live with herself if something happened to him? She asked him to quit and he said he would, but he didn't. So, she had simply left.

Sofie remembered the day he'd asked to meet her before the news broke about Lacey. He'd wanted to tell her first. Before he got to her office, she knew what he was coming to tell her. It was the tone of his voice. As she stood outside her office, he told her that he was sorry he couldn't bring Lacey, her best friend, home to her alive. He told Sofie that he knew how much she wanted that and said that if he could reach into the heavens above and make that miracle happen for her, he would. She knew it, as that was just the kind of man he was.

She fell into his arms and cried. She cried that day for Lacey and for her babies, who would never have the chance to know their mother the way she and Connor had. Truth be told, she also cried for her and Connor. But today she had promised Zackery that she would sing Lacey's favorite song. So, with that, she pulled strength from somewhere down deep inside to sing. Connor could hear her voice from on top of the hill where he was standing. He knew how hard this must be for Sofie.

After Sofie finished her song, Zackery had asked for bagpipers to play *Going Home*. Sofie took her seat as the bagpipes started. Then, as a tear rolled down her cheek, she turned around and watched the man and his dog walk over the hill and out of sight.

-THE END-

A MESSAGE FROM TIM

I hope you enjoyed this book; if so, please help the author! Book reviews are crucial. If you enjoyed reading *Dancing Queen* by Timothy Glass, here are a few things that are vital to the success of any author. To help me, tell others about my books. Word-of-mouth "advertising" is the most powerful marketing tool there is. Statistics show it is better than expensive TV commercials or full-page magazine ads. Also, leaving an honest review is the best way to ensure I will be able to keep writing full-time. I'd greatly appreciate it if you'd consider leaving a rating for the book and writing a brief review. It doesn't have to be long, a sentence or two will help and is all that is needed.

    I would greatly appreciate it.
    Timothy Glass

ABOUT THE AUTHOR

 Timothy Glass was born in Pennsylvania but grew up in Central New Mexico.

Tim was a first responder for almost nine years to earn money to pay for college.

Tim graduated from the University of New Mexico. He later spent some time in New England and central Florida. Glass is an award-winning author, illustrator, cartoonist, and writing instructor. Tim has worked as a ghostwriter and a story consultant.

Glass started his writing career as a journalist under the pen name of C. Stewart. He has written and published more than 400 nonfiction articles nationally and internationally for the health and fitness industry. Glass worked as a regular contributing writer for several New York based magazines. Until the magazine's retirement in the late 1990s, Tim was a freelance journalist for *It's a Wrap* magazine, a New Mexico entertainment quarterly.

VISIT US ON THE WEB

Tim's website: www.timglass.com.

Tim's Cartoons: http://www.timglass.com/Cartoons/

Facebook:
https://www.facebook.com/pages/Timothy-Glass/146746625258?ref=ts

Twitter:
www.twitter.com/timothyglass/

LinkedIn:
http://www.linkedin.com/in/ timothyglass

Instagram:
http://www.instagram.com/timothy.glass

Sleepytown Beagles fabric and wrapping paper:
https://www.spoonflower.com/profiles/sleepytown_beagles

CPSIA information can be obtained
at www.ICGtesting.com
Printed in the USA
LVHW031906090323
741245LV00023B/85

9 781733 197229